THE ALTAR OF HATE

THE ALTAR OF HATE

Vox Day

CASTALIA HOUSE

The Altar of Hate
Vox Day

Published by Castalia House, Switzerland.

Cover by Castalia House
Copyright © 2023 by Vox Day
All Rights Reserved.

ISBN: 978-952-7065-01-3
Version 1

Contents

Raj and Garou

How I wish I could forget the autumn of that fateful year! I was new to India, and like so many unwary Englishmen before me, I was ensnared, my life forever altered by that magical, majestic, and mysterious land. But I was not caught immediately, certainly not when I first arrived on the subcontinent, my two battered suitcases packed near to bursting with t-shirts, textbooks, and a panoply of insect repellants.

Now I have seen the dark reality of that ancient place, and I know why those upon whom the sun never set feared to leave it lurking behind them, out of their iron-fisted control. And yet I am still ashamed to remember that my first thought upon descending from the rickety Air India seven-twenty-seven was one of disgust, my delicate American sensibilities offended by the dirt and the smell. It was unpleasant, it was repellent, and it was bewildering, but I found myself fascinated by the sheer outlandishness of it all.

So very like a Westerner, I hear the good doctor saying even as I pen these words, not with a sneer, but with a smile both wise and wry. He was waiting for me as I deplaned, standing on the cracked and weedy pavement of the tarmac, a short, slender man with the quiet dignity that makes a giant of even the most diminutive gentleman. Dr. Yadvendradev Jhala was his name, and though my knowledge of Hindi grew rapidly in the time I spent with him, I was always glad to keep things formal. Even now, I cannot possibly think of him as anything but Dr. Jhala.

"Welcome to India, Mr. Cattaneo!" he said with a smile.

His English was good, though inflected with the lilting, bird-like intonations so common to sub-continental speakers. His appearance was pleasant rather than handsome, but I liked him at first sight. In the academic world there are many poseurs and pretenders, but Dr. Jhala was not one of them.

He shook my hand, and led me to what was presumably the baggage claim, though it was nothing but a circle chalked upon the asphalt. He was my sponsor for the study program which had brought me here, and although we'd exchanged many emails over the last six months, we'd never met before, nor had we even spoken on the telephone. I held a master's degree in zoology from Columbia, and was in the process of writing my doctoral thesis on the efforts to prevent the extinction of the endangered Bengal tigers, efforts that were primarily in the good doctor's capable hands. He was India's foremost expert on the large predators, and as far as I was concerned, the chance to study under him was the opportunity of a lifetime. And so it proved to be, although not quite in the way I'd imagined.

Dinner that night was rather better than I'd expected. The Indians may be a slender people, but they are not always balanced upon the precipice of starvation. The curried rice was hot and spicy, and we washed it down with a native beer that, while not up to German standards, wasn't bad either. It certainly beat the Stroh's I was normally accustomed to drinking on my limited student's budget.

"You come at an interesting time, Mr. Cattaneo," Dr. Jhala said as he waved off the waiter hovering at his ear.

I raised my eyebrows. It sounded promising, although, of course, 'interesting' could mean almost anything. "Why's that?"

He didn't answer my question directly. Instead, he sipped delicately at his half-empty glass and regarded me thoughtfully. "How familiar are you with the popular legends of the Indian man-killers?" he finally asked.

I smiled. Tiger, tiger, burning bright. "Enough to know that the legends are real, from time to time. When a beast grows old, or is injured, or is simply too sick to pursue its natural prey, it may, upon occasion, turn to humans for its sustenance."

Dr. Jhala nodded. "Yes, although it is certainly the case that crocodiles account for far more deaths than all the big cats of the world combined. Nevertheless, there appears to be something deep within the human psyche that causes us to fear the tiger, particularly here in India, where the risk is real, however slight."

He was clearly leading up to something, and I was pretty sure I knew what it was. A man-killer wouldn't do much for my thesis as currently envisioned, but that could always be changed. In fact, it would almost have to be changed. What an opportunity this could be! I hesitated, then took the plunge.

"Am I correct in guessing that there's one out there right now?"

He nodded, and I slapped the table excitedly, knocking over my water glass in the process. Fortunately, it was empty. I sputtered my apologies, but Dr. Jhala waved them away without concern. I soon forgot my embarrassment, though, as the doctor solemnly confirmed my conjecture.

"It is quite possible indeed. One might even say, probable. There are a number of villages in the Ganges River Basin which have reported a disturbingly large number of attacks. Many children have disappeared during the night, and their bodies have been found later with signs of having been taken for the purposes of... how shall I say this?"

Doctor Jhala paused, and then shook his head sadly.

"No, there is no nice way. The fact is, they have been devoured, either wholly or in part."

I grimaced politely, but inside, I was thrilled. A man-eater! Now that would be a thesis worth writing! Visions of celebrity and an Animal Channel sponsorship began entering my head, unbidden.

"You said a large number of attacks?" I cursed myself for not bringing any note-taking materials with me to the dinner. "How many, exactly?"

"Forty-seven," Dr. Jhala informed me. My jaw dropped. "Thirty-two children have been killed, and fifteen adults. This has been over a period of twenty-four weeks."

Forty-seven people in twenty-four weeks? Holy smokes, that sounded more like a religious massacre up in Kashmir than a man-eating tiger! His words seemed to confirm my subconscious notion of India being a land where life was cheap and the people dropped like flies.

"Adults too, huh? Isn't that a little strange? I guess I just find it hard to believe that a single animal could account for that many attacks."

The doctor nodded.

"It seems unlikely, and yet when you consider the fact that an adult male can be expected to account for one sambok every ten days, it is quite possible. An injured beast hunting easier and smaller prey might well seek out a meal every five days."

"You're sure it's a tiger?"

"No, of course we cannot be sure at this moment. But the most important fact is that the attacks have taken place at night, which is a natural indication of tiger activity. There are those who insist that the large numbers must necessarily indicate that wolves are responsible, but bounty hunters have killed several wolves known to frequent the area, and when I examined their bodies—the wolves, that is, not the hunters, of course—I found no signs to indicate they had been preying upon humans."

I have to admit that I wasn't listening very closely to him at the time. I was so enthused by the prospect of actually studying a man-eater that the doctor's brief dissertation on lupine dissection was lost on me. But in my defense, you should understand that the number of verified cases of large cats intentionally preying on humans is extremely small, and the number of victims here exceeded every case I'd ever heard about, with the possible exception of the notorious Tsavo lions.

My interest in the man-eater may seem morbid to you, but I assure you that I am, and always have been, totally committed to the preservation of wildlife in all its forms. I know that some people might regard my reaction as crass, but you see, if Dr. Jhala's suspicions turned out to be true, then my future as an environmentalist academic was almost certainly assured, leaving me free to devote my efforts to where they would do the most good instead of scrabbling with every other post-graduate in the field for the very few paying jobs that were available. This promised to be an amazing stroke of good fortune!

I can barely remember the rest of the dinner, and although we made an early start the next morning, we couldn't leave soon enough for me. But India is a vast country of poorly-paved roads, I learned to my dismay, and it took us more than a week to reach the village of Anacona, a place that appeared to have been very little affected by the nineteenth century, still less the twentieth. The small huts of the villagers lacked both doors and floors, and despite the recent tragedies there were still an alarming number of filthy, barefooted children running happily about, heedless of any danger.

I spent the first day helping the drivers set up our camp, as Dr. Jhala began the arduous task of interviewing villagers. Unfortunately, we learned very little from the local people, although I was amazed to discover that the beast had grown so bold that it had actually dared to enter several huts under the cover of darkness, on each occasion taking a child off to its doom. The villagers seemed to have a fatalistic attitude about these deaths; like other calamities that had touched their primitive lives, these mysterious deaths simply presented something to be endured.

The bounty hunters were another matter. They were loud and arrogant, slinging loaded thirty-caliber rifles around carelessly as if they were harmless pieces of wood, not deadly weapons liable to go off at any second. I hated being in their company, hated their outlandish moustaches and pseudo-English Gunga Din manners. However, I had little choice in the matter, as I was not yet capable of speaking with the villagers and the hunters were quite conversational in English, for the most part.

Ram Singh was the worst of them. He was a late arrival, having shown up only days before our coming. A big man, surprisingly big for an Indian, he had the powerful shoulders of a home run hitter and the attitude to match. He boasted often of his prowess on the cricket ground, and I, for one, had no trouble believing him. He soon proved to be the most successful of the hunters, and in only three weeks, took five wolves, as many as the rest of the hunters had collected in the previous month combined. His blustery manner concealed what was, beneath the hail-fellow-well-met exterior, a capable and crafty mind.

I despised him for what he was, a ruthless killer with no regard for the noble animals he slew, but I found myself forced to respect his abilities. In this, I followed Dr. Jhala's example, although the two men's argument over the nature of the man-eater continued through the summer's end and well into the autumn.

Dr. Jhala was growing ever more sure that the animal responsible was a tiger, while Ram Singh's conviction that the killer was a wolf remained unshaken. When the body of the eleventh wolf was brought into camp, a big brute with terrible white scars along its side, a likely candidate for a man-killer if I'd ever seen one, even Dr. Jhala began to harbor doubts about the tiger. But electrons don't lie, and when the micrograph proved that even this great monster had never fed upon humans, most of the hunters began to come around to our way of thinking. Not Ram Singh, though.

Since our arrival, another eight children had been taken from five villages in the area, and two adults were missing. The beast seemed to be avoiding Anacona proper, perhaps because of our encampment, which was surrounded by barbed wire and lit brightly by generator-powered search lamps. Dr. Jhala was of the opinion that even a man-killer so bold as this one would not dare to test our camp, and by daylight it was easy to agree with his blithe sensibility. But in that hot and sleepless darkness, I thought of Tsavo and shivered. My mind's eye found it all too easy to picture that terrible duo leaping the high, but ineffective fence, and dragging helpless men screaming from their cots to be devoured noisily, messily, horribly, in the deep shadows of the African night.

As the weeks passed and my nightly terrors grew, I found myself coming to admire these villagers, who, I learned as I spent more time with them, eating meals, washing clothes, and burying the dead, were not ignorant of their danger. Rather, they had come to terms with the knowledge that their lives might end before the dawn, and they had learned that even the most unthinkable loss might be survived. Death, to them, was not the stark finality that I had always believed it to be, instead it was another step on the great circle of that which is and once more will be. How wise they were, and how brave. My fear did not disappear, but at least it did not increase, and it was not too long before I was able to sleep again.

I do not sleep at night now. I do not dare.

It was the fifteenth of October when we caught the killer. Over Dr. Jhala's vociferous protests, Ram Singh had arranged for an impoverished family to move into two houses on the outskirts of Anacona. It was a large family, with four children under the age of five, and the cold-hearted hunter was callously using them as tiger bait. Or wolf bait, as he considered it. Either way, both Dr. Jhala and I were appalled at his methods, as I hope you can imagine.

I was not sitting with Ram Singh that night, but I was having trouble sleeping and I heard the shots, like two corks popping out of a well-shook bottle of champagne. It took me a moment to realize what the sounds meant, but as soon as my fogged brain came to the correct conclusion, I leaped from my cot and ran towards the stand the hunter had been using. I reached it only a step or two before Dr. Jhala, and both of us nearly stumbled over Ram Singh, who was crouched beside the tree trunk.

He held up a finger, stained dark in the scanty light provided by my flashlight.

"I hit him at least once. In the shoulder, I think. He won't make it far. Let's find him!"

"What was it?"

The hunter smiled at the doctor.

"You'll see very soon, I imagine. But I'm right, you know."

His arrogant certainty irritated me, and I hoped very much that he was wrong. But he wasn't. Not one hundred paces away, we discovered the motionless body of the largest wolf I have ever seen in my life. It was massive, the size of a small bear, and it had not died easily. Its teeth were bared in a rictus snarl of hateful defiance, and for the first time I found myself doubting my belief that animals are innocent in their savagery, wholly outside the realm of good and evil.

"Hit him with both shots," Singh said with satisfaction in his voice. "How about that?"

He was almost gleeful, mad with joy. For a moment, I had the terrible impression that he was about to dance a victory jig, like Hitler at Versailles.

"So much for the tiger," I said, my dreams of a career with the Animal Channel as dead as the monster lying before us. This killer would only be a matter of academic interest to anyone back home. A wolf, even a monster such as this, simply didn't have the majestic size, the dangerous cachet, to be worthy of the dread label "man-eater," no matter how many people it had slain.

"I hope so," said Dr. Jhala, much to my surprise.

He seemed dubious, somehow, that we'd really caught the killer. I didn't understand why, not at the time, but he had his reasons. Ram Singh and I helped him lug the big brute back to his makeshift laboratory, after which, despite the late hour, Dr. Jhala began the autopsy. I would have liked nothing better than to return to my bed, as all the energy induced by the excitement had worn off, but I was determined to assist him. By the time the sun rose, no doubts remained. The great wolf was indeed our man-killer. Our long hunt was over, and the people of Anacona were finally safe.

I was surprised to discover the doctor back at the micrograph following dinner the next evening. He seemed worried, and more than a little perplexed. Removing a sample from the little machine, he replaced it with another, examined it, then sighed and pushed himself away from the table at which he was sitting.

"What's the matter?"

He stared at me as if he didn't know who I was for a second, then rubbed at his temples and shook his head.

"I wish I could say. But there are simply no anomalies… and yet it makes no sense otherwise… But there must be a reason!"

I had no idea what he was getting at. I pressed him for an explanation, but none was forthcoming. He refused to even hint at his suspicions, whatever they were, but he did admit that whatever was bothering him bore no connection to the wolf Ram Singh had killed the night before. The man-killer was well and truly dead, and our work here was done.

The people of the village did their best to thank us, and held a dinner in our honor which only made me feel guilty that we hadn't caught the killer sooner. Ram Singh and his fellow hunters felt no shame, though, and they were more than happy to join the villagers in vigorously drinking each another's health. Dr. Jhala was strangely withdrawn into himself, and more than once I caught him staring off into the jungle, with a pensive expression on his face.

He left early, while I stuck around for another round or two of warm Indian beer before turning in. Unlike the night before, I had no trouble falling asleep, and was sleeping the sleep of the reasonably drunk when my dreams were interrupted by an unpleasant commotion. It sounded nearby, but it wasn't until I heard the distinctive crunch of glass being ground underfoot that I realized something was going on in the laboratory.

I burst through the canvas flaps of the tent, and my breath caught in my throat as I saw the destruction that had been wrought there. Everything was smashed, tables were turned over, the laptop screen was shattered, and notepaper lay scattered all about like a thin covering of snow. The light was dim, and so it took me several minutes to notice Dr. Jhala lying partially hidden by an overturned chair. He was dead, his chest crushed by a powerful blow from a blunt instrument. I choked back a scream, and forced myself to look more closely.

The poor doctor's face was scored deeply by four parallel lines, and it occurred to me that the massive wound in his chest could have been caused by a large paw. A tiger's paw? It seemed possible. But we'd already determined that the wolf had been the killer, that there never had been a tiger in the first place! Then I noticed something strange beside the doctor's body. Not far from his right hand, lying there as if he'd dropped it, was a revolver. In checking to see if it was loaded, which it was, I saw that the unjacketed bullets in the chambers were shiny, not dark. They were silver.

I rose to my feet, turned around, and froze. Not twenty feet away was the tiger, a big one, perhaps fifteen feet in length. Its eyes were yellow, and startlingly intelligent. It growled threateningly, but fell silent as I snapped the cylinder shut and pointed the weapon at its face.

"I don't know what's going on here, but if you can understand me, then I expect you understand what it means that this gun is loaded with silver bullets."

The great beast simply stared at me, unblinking.

"Okay, so maybe my imagination is running away with me. I guess if you're just an animal, then that won't mean anything to you."

I cocked the hammer with my thumb.

The tiger blinked once. Then it was gone, like a shadow in the darkness. It left me there, alone and shaking, with the doctor's mutilated corpse.

It was too late to do anything for Dr. Jhala. But if nothing else, I had to solve the mystery of his death. Still holding the gun in my hand, fearing the tiger's return, I flicked on a stationary flashlight and began to gather the doctor's notes, quickly perusing them as I did so. I had stacked perhaps twenty pieces of paper in a little pile when I found it, three short lines written in Dr. Jhala's precise hand. It proved nothing, except that I wasn't the only one with an imagination.

two bullets

1 –pierced and broke shoulder 2 –penetrated heart, lethal shot

both silver!!!! why?????

The word 'why' was underlined three times. So that was what was bothering the poor doctor. Ram Singh's rifle, the one with which he killed the wolf, had been loaded with silver. If my dreadful suspicions were correct, he had done so in the full knowledge that what he hunted was not a normal wolf. But that necessarily didn't make him, what, a weretiger? I'd never heard of such a thing, not even in the movies!

But there was no denying two things. Dr. Jhala was dead, and something had killed him. Something that understood silver to be a particular danger to it.

I heard footsteps rapidly approaching, someone running towards the tent. Ram Singh pushed his way inside, dressed as if he'd come from his bed and holding his thirty ought six.

"I heard a noise. What the hell happened here?"

His eyes, a dark, but very human shade of brown, were open wide with surprise as he glanced around the disheveled interior of the tent. Then he froze, and his mouth dropped open when he saw the blood, and the body of the unfortunate doctor. A look of horror filled his face.

Or so he thought. He was a terrible actor. I'd seen more genuine shock and astonishment in my high school acting class.

I lifted the revolver with both hands, pointing it at his chest.

"Drop it!"

He obeyed quickly, laying his rifle upon the ground, still affecting surprise.

"What's the matter with you? What happened to him?"

"I imagine you know more about that than I do. There really is silver in this thing, by the way. Dr. Jhala must have been on to you, which is probably why you killed him."

"Nonsense!" The powerfully-built hunter scoffed, but his eyes were hard, and calculating. "Don't you think you'll have a hard time explaining why you shot me, old chap? This ridiculous notion of silver bullets and, I presume, werewolves, aside, I can't imagine you'd relish the notion of spending time in an Indian prison."

I kept a straight face, but shuddered inside. He had a point. I wasn't after justice or revenge, I just wanted to get out of there, leave that dark and terrible country.

"Dr. Jhala was my friend," I answered. "I know you killed him. But I can't prove anything, so now I just want to get out of this stinking place. In one piece."

"Then go." He smiled, his teeth white against his dark face, and gestured towards the tent flap. "By all means."

"I want to know why. Why you killed him."

"I can't tell you that. I didn't kill him."

"Then tell me why your gun was loaded with silver."

"It's an affectation."

"Like the mustache?"

He glared at me.

We were getting nowhere with this, I decided. Maybe my suspicions were wrong, or maybe not, but he clearly wasn't about to confess his sins to me. So be it. I wanted answers, but not enough to risk my life chasing them. I ordered him to kick the rifle towards me, and then carefully picked it up. Keeping both weapons trained on him, I forced him to move away from the entrance and towards the rear of the tent as I backed out of it.

Once outside, I sprinted towards the closest jeep. I wasted no time fetching my belongings, and my wallet, with the meager funds it contained, was already in my pocket. I tossed Singh's rifle in the back of the jeep and kept the revolver in my hand, nervously looking about as the ancient engine coughed its way to life. As I shifted into reverse, the headlights caught a pair of yellow eyes staring at me from the darkness, some distance away. Was it the tiger? Was it Ram Singh? Or was it the two in one? I didn't wait to find out.

I caught the first flight from New Dehli, not the least bit concerned about the ruinous expense of a last-minute ticket. Like the Empire, I am gone, never to return to that frightening and perilous land. Werewolves, weretigers, I want no part of their unseen war, and one glance beyond the veil was one more than I wanted. But my eyes have been opened, and even here, ensconced in the comfortable environment that is everyday life in America, I have seen things that I, as a man of science, cannot properly explain.

A glimpse of an oversized dog in Atlanta. A catfight in Los Angeles, hair-raising yowls interspersed with the clash of metal on metal. A tall, slender girl in San Francisco, her eyes gleaming too-brightly in the shadows of the moonlight, and her smile, the anticipatory grin of the predator.

I have kept my silence, though, and with it, my career. There is no Animal Channel, but I am paid reasonably well to work the night shift, caring for the great cats that spend their languid days at the Minnesota Zoo. And if the bullets in the revolver which I carry at all times are made of silver, well, what of it? It is an affectation, nothing more.

A Reliable Source

Even with the drone's high-resolution camera, the streamed video appeared blurry at the edges on the massive high-definition screen in the middle of the Operations Center. The GPS coordinates across the bottom were sharp and clear, however. Just moments ago, three men exited the building over which the camera sights had been hovering and climbed into a white Jeep Grand Cherokee that was parked near the side entrance. No sooner had the third man closed the rear driver-side door than the vehicle disappeared in a flash of bright light, followed by a billowing cloud of white smoke.

"Bang, you're dead," a young 2nd lieutenant cried exultantly.

"Settle down, Wexsler," barked Captain Hainesworth. He glanced at Ronald, who was too busy frowning at some notes he'd marked on legal pad from an earlier briefing to have noticed the lieutenant's outburst. "Sorry, Colonel."

"What's that?" Colonel Ronald M. James, Wing Commander of the 111th Fighter Wing, wasn't paying attention. "That's a confirmed kill. No question concerning the identities of the three targets?"

"None whatsoever, Colonel. We had solid intel from NSA."

"Very good, Captain. Who was flying?"

"Major McGinness was the pilot, sir."

"A nice clean kill. No collateral damage. That's what I like to see." Ronald scribbled a brief note on his pad, reminding himself to review the After Action Report and put the captain in for a medal. He was overdue. "Tell the major I said as much."

"Of course, Colonel."

The three militants never had a chance. The MQ-13 Grimm could carry 1,500 pounds of ordnance, which usually took the form of GBU-42 PLH bombs and AGM-117 Hellfire III air-to-ground missiles. It was also equipped with a pair of mini-ATAS missiles and an XM-2 autofletchette for defense against enemy drones. It could stay in the air for 96 hours, floating patiently high above its unknowing targets, waiting until the right opportunity presented itself.

Judging by the size of the explosion, the white vehicle had been taken out by a Hellfire. And just like that, Ronald could scratch two more names off the Pentagon's list of most wanted militants. Which was certainly timely, considering his meeting in Washington this afternoon; being able to report the kills in person to the Commander of Strategic Air-To-Ground Operations, more commonly known as SATGO, would be one more checked box on his eventual ticket out of Willow Grove. The mission had actually been completed several hours ago, before he'd even arrived in the op center, but he'd wanted to personally review the recording before he departed in case he was asked any questions about it.

Not that he minded life in the suburban Pennsylvania town. Jennifer enjoyed its proximity to the civilized amenities of Philadelphia and the public schools were a damned sight better than they'd been on his last two assignments. Bruce was the proud third-string defensive end on the junior high football team and Michaela was active in gymnastics as well as some sort of knitting group, if he understood correctly.

But the fact was that the 111th Fighter Wing was an Air Guard unit, not a proper Air Force unit, its manned aircraft had been permanently grounded seven years ago, and an air base located out in the middle of suburban Pennsylvania was no place to win a general's stars. He'd made full bird four years ago and leaped at the chance to command the UAV base established there because he knew drones were the future of air combat. But since then, he'd learned that the promotions and plum assignments were still mostly going to the traditional flyboys commanding bomber wings and the sort of fighter wings that still had real planes and pilots.

Tradition was always hard to overcome. But things were changing. The 111th now had 25 Reapers and 10 Grimms in the place of the A-10 Thunderbolts it had once flown, and had used them to rack up more confirmed kills in the last year than any traditional fighter wing in the Air Force. Targeted drone strikes might be considerably less glamorous than high-altitude bombing or dogfighting, but no one could deny that they were a damned sight more useful these days in light of the understandable reluctance of the Red Chinese, the Russians, or anyone else to challenge American air supremacy.

And under his command, the 111th boasted the third highest kill rate per mission of the 72 drone bases around the country. Perhaps more impressively, his operators had only lost one bird, an old model Global Hawk that was hacked and diverted by unknown parties while flying over Ghana. Ronald assumed it was the Chinese, since no one ever took credit for the exploit and neither the Iranians nor the jihadists were inclined to keep their mouths shut whenever they seized a drone.

"Sir, your plane is ready," a lieutenant informed him.

He nodded. "Remind Bart that I won't be back until Monday, Eric." Bart was Colonel Corbett, the wing's Vice Commander and Ronald's second-in-command.

"Will do, Colonel. Have a safe trip." Captain Hainesworth saluted crisply and Ronald acknowledged it. He stopped by his office long enough to slip the legal pad into his attaché, tucked his lid under his arm, and made his way out to the tarmac. One benefit of commanding an Air Force base, even if it was a fighter wing without any fighters, was having ready access to air transportation.

The T-6A Texan II, one of the base's two trainers, was already warmed up and waiting for him. The Beechcraft was no speed demon, but it would get him to Fort Drum before he would even have been able to board a commercial flight in Philadelphia. His garment bag was already stowed underneath, so he gave the pilot, a captain by the name of John Hallowell, a thumb's up as soon as he was strapped in.

Ronald would have preferred to fly himself, but these flights were too good an opportunity to see how the younger officers comported themselves to pass up. And it was nice to relax in the back seat, knowing that no one would ambush him with questions or urgent matters requiring immediate resolution. The skies were clear, the takeoff was smooth, and Hallowell proved to be pleasantly taciturn. They had barely reached cruising altitude before Ronald fell asleep.

Fort Drum was considerably busier than Horsham and its security was much tighter. Once they were on the ground, he and Hallowell were met by a pair of muscular infantrymen, who escorted Ronald to a black Suburban that ferried him to an unexpectedly beautiful cream-colored mansion featuring four massive white pillars in the front. There he was greeted by an Army colonel, his garment bag was collected by a lieutenant, and he was shown into a well-appointed, high-ceilinged meeting room in which there were eleven officers wearing the uniforms of four different service branches.

There were four other Air Force men, one general and three colonels, five Army generals, one rear admiral, and a short Marine general who looked rather like the bulldog that served as his Corps's mascot. He didn't recognize most of them, but he knew they were his counterparts, commanders of various drone bases from Florida to Alaska.

"There's the man of the hour!" General William Norstad, commander of SATGO, was a tall man whose broad shoulders bore three stars apiece. "Colonel James, allow me to be the first to congratulate you. And someone get this man a beer!"

"Thank you, General." James smiled at the blank looks on the faces of the men from the other three forces. "We had some first-rate support from the intelligence community."

"Earlier this morning, a Grimm pilot under Colonel James's command terminated with what can only be described as extreme prejudice both Aden al-Muhajir and Osama al-Ansari, numbers twelve and eighteen on our priority list."

"Just doing our job, General." The officers with their hands free clapped, others raised their drinks in salute. Three more officers arrived, including another Air Force general, and they, too, came over to congratulate James and shake his hand as the reason for the celebratory mood was explained to them.

However, once all sixteen of the invited commanders were present, Norstad's face grew more serious and he urged them all to take a seat and get comfortable.

"I'm sure most of you are wondering what the purpose of this interservice conclave is. As I expect you will have worked out by now, all of you command drone bases located on U.S. soil. As it happens, you represent sixteen of the twenty-five most effective drone commands in terms of kill-to-mission ratio. I think it speaks well of the armed forces that each branch is represented here today; it appears excellence in unmanned flight operations is not limited to the U.S. Air Force!"

There were a few groans at this, but in light of Norstad's compliments, the officers from the other service branches were inclined to let the little dig go.

"However, the nature of war is such that no success long goes unremarked by the enemy. As with the laws of physics, for every action there is bound to be a reaction of some kind. In the last four years, our drones have successfully targeted over fifty-six hundred enemy combatants and proven to be our most effective weapon in the ongoing effort against terrorists and militant extremists around the globe. So, it is not surprising that the enemy appears to have embarked upon a new strategy, one that involves attacking our drone pilots and sensor operators here in the United States of America!"

There was more than a little murmuring at this, but James exchanged a glance with the Marine general, who nodded at him, his face showing absolutely no surprise. Had the Marines lost any pilots, or was this simply the Corps's storied stoicism in action?

"In the last six months, fourteen drone pilots and three sensor operators have been found dead in circumstances ranging from deeply suspicious to seemingly innocuous. In addition, eight non-flying staff officers have either been murdered or committed suicide, inexplicably in the case of the latter. These deaths fall within the range of statistical probability, athough they are on the high side, and none of them show any overt signs of being the result of terrorist activity. Moreover, the 25 deaths were spread out among twenty different bases, which is why no one recognized the pattern until there was a reason to go looking for it."

"What sort of reason was that, General?"

Norstad smiled grimly and turned to face the Army general who'd asked the question. "Two weeks ago, the National Security Agency contacted SATGO with regards to intel it harvested from a social media site. We were informed that a YouTube channel was being used by a militant branch of Parisian jihadists to disseminate coded messages in retro music videos, hiding their communications in plain sight. Apparently single frames consisting of one letter were being inserted into the videos, which were invisible at a normal 24 frames-per-second rate, but allowed the viewer to read the message when the video was slowed down."

"Are you're saying that a connection between some of these deaths and the YouTube videos has been established? Or is this just civilian conjecture?" The admiral from Pax River sounded skeptical.

"All the videos associated with that channel have been analyzed. They contained direct references to eighteen of the twenty bases previously mentioned."

And with that, the room fell into stunned silence. Norstad nodded. "We are no longer the predators, gentlemen, we are now the prey. In consultation with the NSA and the FBI, SATGO is in the process of developing an enhanced security protocol for all drone bases, foreign and domestic, with a particular emphasis on the bases deemed to be at the greatest risk. I assume you grasp, gentlemen, that your own bases are most certainly among those most likely to be targeted."

"How many of those twenty bases that have already been hit are represented here, General?"

Norstad gave the Marine general a tight smile. "Twelve of them, General. Twelve of them."

That provoked a mild uproar of protest and disbelief. "That's not possible!" "It was a car accident!" "The coroner's report was inconclusive!" Norstad quelled them by raising his hand.

"You see what we are up against. Even when faced with circumstantial evidence of enemy action, you find it hard to believe. Now, perhaps there are some elements of coincidence in play here, but the FBI, with the assistance of both CID and NCIS, is investigating each of the 25 cases and will do its best to either confirm or reject the apparent connection between the militants' videos and the deaths of the base personnel."

James was wracking his brain to see if he could recall any deaths among the service personnel at Horsham. One staff sergeant had been in a fairly serious car accident, but it wasn't a fatal one. And he certainly hadn't lost any pilots or operators, they were woefully understaffed and losing one would have not only forced him to reschedule the flight roster, but cut down on the number of missions they were flying. No, he concluded, his

command was not among the twelve that had been—may have been
—targeted.

Even so, it was a frightening thought. As a consequence of viewing
hundreds of hours of camera footage filmed over cities from Accra to
London, he knew much better than most how the militants moved
invisibly through the innocent crowds at will. And while it might be a
little harder to infiltrate a predominantly white suburban community
like Willow Grove than the banlieues of Paris, Willow Grove was
only twenty miles away from Philadelphia and neighborhoods where
an African jihadist would attract considerably less attention from the
average resident than James himself.

The rest of the conclave consisted of a brainstorming session
concerning how they could beef up security for their personnel, how
much information could reasonably be released to both personnel
and public without causing unnecessary panic, and an idea for an
interservice line of communications for reporting any incidents that
might indicate militant activity was outlined. But they all knew they
were doing little more than whistling through the graveyard. As
the shootings at Fort Hood, Quantico, and the Navy Yard proved,
it was impossible to eliminate the dangers posed by a determined
killer.

Two hours later, James was offered a ride back to his plane by
General Norstad, who had his own plane on standby.

"You kept your thoughts to yourself in there, Ron," the general
observed.

"It's not that I'm not grateful for the warning, General. I'm just
dubious that we'll be able to do much more than pick up the pieces
afterward."

"You're right. In fact, several members of my staff were very
strongly of the opinion that we should simply leave you all in the
dark. But my thinking is that if there is a solution to be found, the

sort of men who were in that room are the men most likely to find it." He met James's eyes and nodded. "I asked you to ride along for a reason. First, to tell you to call me Bill. I think we're going to be working together more often in the future and you may as well get used to it. Second, I want to ask you if you think you're ready to keep more than 35 birds in the air."

"Sir?"

"Jim Cooper will be on the next general's list. He's moving on from Creech to a command in Europe six weeks from now. That means the 432nd Wing is in need of a commander."

James blinked, astonished. The 432nd was the Air Force's premier UAV wing, with five times more drones than the 111th and nearly 500 aircrew members. It wasn't so much a step up as a great leap forward. "You want to give me the 432nd?"

"I think you're the man for it, Ron. However, there's just one catch."

Of course there was. "What's that?"

"I want you to head up that interservice communication system we discussed. Nothing official, you understand. If we try to make it formal then it will wind up having to go through the Joint Chiefs and it will be two years before anyone can tell anyone else what he had for breakfast. But a regular flow of scuttlebutt between base commanders about any car accidents or steel-jacketed lead overdoses, with someone keeping notes, might be extremely useful if our friends at the NSA happen to be correct about the opfor bringing the battle to us."

James nodded. It made sense. And he understood the reason for the catch too. A pissant colonel on an Air Guard base didn't have the juice to be at the center of that sort of informal network. But the commander of the 432nd undoubtedly did. And if he didn't screw up, there was every chance that he'd get his star sooner rather than not at all.

He took a deep breath. "I'll be glad to do it, Bill. If you think I can do it, then I'm your man."

The general extended his hand and smiled. "I don't think you can, Ron. I know you can."

"How was your meeting, honey?" He didn't know if it was his good mood or not, but Jennifer was looking particularly vivacious in her t-shirt and jeans as she greeted him in the kitchen.

"It was... interesting. They have unusual opinions on base housing, to say the least. How do you feel about Nevada?"

"Nevada? I don't know that I've ever thought about it." She frowned. Then her eyes widened. "You don't mean Creech!"

He grinned. "That's exactly what I mean."

"Oh, honey!" She leaped into his arms. "That's wonderful!"

He laughed, and carefully disengaged himself from her. "It's not official yet. And it doesn't necessarily mean I'll make flag rank."

"But it means you probably will?"

"If I don't manage to screw up by dropping a Hellfire on Windsor Castle or something, yeah, I probably will."

"Ha!" she exclaimed and kissed him enthusiastically. "I told Bonnie you'd get your first star before Robert did."

"It's not a competition!"

"Don't be silly, Ron. Everything is a competition. Especially among military wives. You have no idea how many condescending women were reassuring me after you took this command instead of staying on at Beale. What unit are they giving you?"

"The 432nd. It has 245 birds, and 488 pilots and operators. Another 350 maintenance personnel, plus the usual catalog of contractors. It's a pretty big step up from here. Bigger than I'd anticipated, to be honest."

"Wow," she marveled. She pounded his chest with her open palm. "This calls for a celebration, Colonel James! How do you feel about steaks?"

"I feel very strongly that they should be preceded by a bottle of beer," he said, opening the refrigerator. "Possibly two. And, by the way, not one word to the kids, not until it's settled. I don't want to upset them in case it turns out to be a false alarm."

"Oh, God," she said, "the kids! Bruce will be all right now that the football season is over, but Michaela will be devastated!"

"She'll be all right," James reassured her. "She's a tough kid and this is hardly the first time we've moved."

It was ten days before his official notification was scheduled to arrive. He and Jennifer had done what they could to prepare the children for the possibility that they would be leaving Willow Grove, but any guilt that he felt over uprooting them again was drowned out by his excitement at the challenge of overseeing up to twenty missions per day. He'd reviewed as much material from Creech as he could quietly obtain from his various connections around the Air Force, and from what he'd gleaned, both on and off the record, was that the former Colonel Cooper's methods left a good bit of room for improvement. The 432nd's kill-to-mission rate wasn't bad for such a large operation, although it was less than half that of the 111th, but it soon became clear that Cooper was a bit of a cowboy who wasn't terribly averse to collateral damage.

James winced as he read about a school in Kurdistan, a church mistaken for a mosque in Nigeria, and a blue-on-blue incident that took the lives of three Marines in Iraq. Such incidents were tragic, but worse, they were absolutely unnecessary. It was clear that a little patience on the part of the pilot would have sufficed to avoid each of the three incidents. Such failures, he knew, were down to the commander and the atmosphere he'd constructed. And although it was painful to review the details of the various collaterals, the mistakes did give him confidence that he would be able to prove worthy of General Norstad's trust and improve the unit's performance.

He was being driven home from the base by Mike Hernandez, his driver for the last three months, when he noticed that the car was not traveling on its customary route. He looked out the window, a little confused as to why the corporal had turned off the main road, and didn't recognize the neighborhood.

"What's going on, Corporal."

"Traffic detour, Colonel," Hernandez answered, his eyes never leaving the road.

That made sense, James thought, although he hadn't noticed any of the customary orange signs. But he began to grow suspicious that something was amiss when Hernandez abruptly pulled into an elementary school parking lot without warning. The lot was empty except for a white Ford, against which a short, slender man wearing a Phillies cap was casually leaning.

"Mike?"

"This man wants to talk to you, Colonel. I understand it's very important."

"What the hell is this, Mike? I don't give a damn what he wants–"

For the first time, Hernandez turned to look into the back seat and James recoiled from the unexpectedly arrogant look in the man's dark eyes. "Shut your mouth, Colonel. Now, get out of the car and talk to the man. He's waiting for you."

James felt the cold sensation of fear enter his body. What was wrong with Hernandez? Had he been subverted? It was worrisome, but somehow, this didn't feel like an assassination attempt. He took a deep breath, then opened the door and stepped out of the car. Hernandez got out too, but he did not follow.

The man wearing the baseball cap smiled and held up a tablet. He was dark-skinned and handsome, with hawkish features. "Good evening, Colonel James. You will excuse the interruption, I hope. I have something to show you, Colonel. You will find it of interest, I think."

"All right. Who are you? What's your name?"

"You can call me David." The man tapped the tablet. "Here, have a look."

James glanced at the image on the screen and froze. It was a picture of Bruce at football practice, and judging by the angle, it had been taken from inside his school.

"Go ahead, just flick your finger across it. It's a touch screen. I'm sure you know how they work."

His heart in his mouth, James flicked past one, two, three, pictures of his children as they went about their day. Four, five, six. There were pictures at school, at the mall, and even in their back yard. Some were as recent as last week.

"Are they..." he couldn't bring himself to finish the sentence. "Did you—"

"Your children are perfectly safe, Colonel. For the moment. However, there is one more thing you need to see." He took back the tablet from James's nerveless hands and tapped it a few times. "There. Have a look."

James knew what it was at once. He had seen too many live videostreams not to recognize one now. It was Jennifer in the kitchen, engaged in making something that involved her mixing bowl. Cookies, most likely. The image was shaking slightly; it was being shot with a handheld camera.

"We are rather less well-equipped than your fine United States Air Force," David said. "But you are a fighting man, for all that you fight like a coward from on high. You know a bullet will kill as effectively as a bomb. It is poetic justice, is it not? You watch us from afar, we watch you from very close by."

James stared at the image of his wife, who appeared to be singing cheerfully along with the radio. "You don't intend to kill me. Or her. You want something from me, don't you."

David smiled. His teeth were very white against his skin. He was clearly of Arab descent, although his accent appeared to indicate that he was a native French speaker. Algerian, perhaps?

"We just want you to do your job, Colonel. That's all. Every now and then, and not so often that it will draw attention to you, you are going to receive intelligence. Reliable intel, very solid intel, complete with names, dates, times, and GPS coordinates. All that is required of you is to do your job and ensure that the package is delivered in a timely manner."

"The package?"

"Don't play stupid now. The bomb. The missile. The bolt of lightning that falls from above and deals death to the innocent and the guilty alike. We will choose the target. And you, you will simply do your job."

"If I refuse, you will kill my wife."

David spread his hands. "We will start with her, at any rate. Do you see my friend here?" He pointed to the man in the driver's seat.

"Yes."

"He is waiting to send a text message. If I tell him you will cooperate, you will go home to your pretty blonde wife. If you do not agree to cooperate, you will go home to her corpse. There is another man accompanying the man with the camera. He has a rifle. You have a choice, Colonel. You will agree to do as we demand or she will die right now."

James closed his eyes. It was one thing to give your life for your country. He was willing to do that. But his wife? She had taken no oath except to love, honor, and obey him. And it would not end with her. These monsters would only target his children next. He realized his only option was to play along, just for the time being.

"All right. Don't hurt her! I'll do what you want."

"Swear it," David demanded.

"I swear," he lied.

"Swear it by your Christian god!"

"I swear it, damn you," he hissed. "I swear it by God! I swear it by everything!"

David relaxed and nodded in a friendly manner. "Very good, Colonel. Very wise. You shall hear from us in time."

"How will I know it is you?"

David flashed his white teeth again, leaving James with no doubt who was the predator and who was the prey. "Oh, you will know, Colonel. Have no fear. You will know. But I warn you, do not listen to Shaitan's whispers, do not be tempted into thinking you can fool us."

"It's not going to work!" James protested.

"Of course it will work, Colonel James. You wish to kill terrorists, do you not? We will give you your terrorists on a silver plate. They will be bad men, very bad men, exactly the sort of men you are already seeking to kill. And what is the enemy of one's enemy, but a friend?"

"Friends don't threaten their friend's families!"

"If you do as you should, your family will come to no harm at all." David's eyes narrowed and grew cold. "But when tomorrow comes and you wake with your wife sleeping soundly beside you, when you begin to think of this moment as nothing more than a bad dream, when you think to confess everything to your superiors and hide behind the walls and guns of the U.S. military, remember who picked you up at your home in the morning and who drove you back again at night. Remember what uniform he wore. We are everywhere, Colonel. We are in your bases and in your homes and in your schools, and there is nowhere you can hide that we cannot reach."

He indicated Hernandez. "When we leave this parking lot, Miguel Hernandez will cease to exist. But there will be other Miguels, here, in Nevada, and in every place you go after that."

"You know about Nevada?"

"Of course, Colonel. You are a precious asset to us. You are the sword with which we will smite our enemies. Your every breath is of great interest to us." With that, David snapped the tablet cover shut, and beckoned to Hernandez, or whatever his name truly was. "So keep your mouth shut and do your job, Colonel, and all will be well with you and yours. Peace be upon you."

He got into the passenger seat of the white car and the driver started the engine. As he walked past James, Mike Hernandez flipped him an ironic salute. "Keys are in the ignition, Colonel. You made the right call. Enjoy your evening with Mrs. James. She's a nice lady."

"Damn you, Mike! You can't think you'll get away with this!" James couldn't help himself.

Hernandez paused as he opened the rear door. "I already have, Colonel. By the time you can get anyone at the FBI or the CIA to take you seriously, I'll be out of the country for good. Mike Hernandez doesn't exist. He never did."

He got into the back seat, slammed the door, and James watched in despair as the white Ford Fusion drive away.

"Are you all right, honey? You look as if you've seen a ghost!"

James didn't say anything. He took her in his arms and held her tightly, inhaling her sweet, familiar scent. How was it possible that he might have lost her not half an hour ago? But she was alive and that was all that mattered. Tomorrow he would think about his options. Tomorrow he would decide what he should do. He'd agreed to do as the bastards demanded, but no forced vow could ever be considered binding. Tonight, however, he was not going to think about anything, tonight he was simply going to be grateful that his family was alive and unharmed.

"Hey, let me go,"she complained. "I've got to get another batch out of the oven. Don't take more than two, Michaela is bringing them to a gymnastics party tonight. Oh, and by the way, she said she has something for you."

He felt as if his blood had suddenly turned to ice. "She did? From who?"

"A note from one of her teachers, I think." She pointed to the counter. "I don't know, open it and see. It's right there."

It was a little cream envelope. 'Colonel Ronald James, USAF' was written on it in a neat female hand.

And James knew there would be no escaping them. Not here, not in Nevada, not anywhere.

The enemy was here. The enemy was hiding in plain sight all around them. The enemy was in the neighborhoods, the schools, the airports, the fast food restaurants, and the shopping malls, and he could no more hide from them than al-Muhajir and al-Ansari had been able to hide from the MQ-13 Grimm soaring silently through the cloudless sky above them.

He slipped the envelope into his pocket.

"What was it, honey?"

"Nothing much," he said. "I'll take care of it tomorrow."

The Lesser Evil

The master sat before us, clenching his gnarled hand into a fist as he banished the last of the magical visions he had created for our edification. His dark hood slipped down to reveal a head that was hairless, and the parchment-like skin stretched delicately across his rounded skull as he leaned back slowly. He exhaled once, deeply. His robes of sumptuous black velvet rustled softly as he turned to face us, and his ancient eyes gleamed like emeralds.

"Power," he whispered harshly, "is the unholiest of grails. Men seek it nonetheless. For some the quest is simply blind instinct, whereas for others it is the dedication of a lifetime."

He paused for a moment to consider the eager face of young Aeris and nodded approvingly.

"You are here because you have the desire, and the talent too. But you must never forget that the pursuit of the grail can kill you, and as the knights of old discovered, even the successful quest may prove fatal."

He fell silent for a moment and examined his wizened fingers, which ended in long, claw-like nails, seemingly forgetting our presence. After a time he looked up at us, his students, holding each of us in turn in that eerie serpentine gaze. Then he spoke again.

"You have heard of the wizard Tetradates," he stated. We surely had.

"Tetradates!" Ganelos, the senior apprentice, was the first to speak, expressing the delight that filled us all. "The Darkmage who summoned the demon Ravana! Did you know him?"

The old one was amused at our excitement.

"He did not actually… summon Baal-Ravana, but yes, I knew him well. I had him killed, you see."

His bloodless lips twisted into a thin smile of dark humor, and he pointed a dessicated finger at the four of us.

"I will tell you the story, and perhaps it will provide you with some small enlightenment."

Aeris leaned back to rest against my knees and we listened as the master's dry voice wove a spell that took us back to a time long past, a time before the Desecration.

A large man sits hulking in front of a television screen, his piggy eyes encased in sagging folds of flesh. He stares intently at the monochromatic images moving silently before him. He waves his hand in an obscure motion that could be an arcane gesture, and he grunts with satisfaction as the voices of the tiny figures become audible. As he eases his bulk into an overloaded leather chair and searches the greasy bottom of a bargain-brand potato-chip bag for edible remnants, a casual observer might easily miss the fact that the end of the old TV's power cord lies nearly a hands-length away from the nearest electrical outlet.

"I've broken oath to come here!" a young man stated icily, as he glared at the men surrounding him. "This is an emergency!"

The speaker was a tall Nordic-looking youth, dressed casually in a tight white t-shirt and torn blue jeans. He was handsome despite the two parallel scars that marred his left cheekbone. He stood in a small room with hardwood floors in front of eight older men, all of whom were clad in flowing white robes and demonstrating varying degrees of interest. A tall grey-bearded man who'd been surveying the young man with a skeptical eye glanced down to examine his exquisitely manicured fingernails.

"So? What is a broken oath among Discordians to us?" he said dismissively, spreading his long white hands palms-upward in an elegant gesture of dismissal. "If you intend to mend your ways, well and good, I suppose, but I don't think the repentance of a minor black-robe calls for the assembly of these august personages."

He sniffed daintily and turned his haughty face towards a man with a shaven head.

"I should say it's been interesting, Gorean, but it hasn't. So I won't."

The bald man smiled slightly. He was a patient man, but even he found the other's arrogant lack of manners difficult to tolerate.

"Ill-spoken as ever, Alexi," he rebuked his colleague, without noticeable effect. "Regardless, I think you will all be interested to hear what the boy has to say, that is, if you will only take the time to listen."

His green-eyed gaze swept across the haughty faces of the others, Masters all, secure in their knowledge and proud in their power.

"Speak on, Dag," he urged the scar-faced youth.

The young man nodded gratefully to his benefactor and turned to face the assembled adepts, his eyes narrowing.

"My news is this. My master, the archmage Tetradates, has made compact with a Duke of the Sixth Hell. The compact was sealed with the great binding Words of Fire and Blood!"

The fat man tosses aside the empty potato-chip bag and smashes a fist against the chair in anger as he lurches ponderously to his feet. The black-and-white image on the screen shows a room full of robed men erupting in consternation around a slender young man, then fades to a spark and disappears. Dozens of dusty, leather-bound books fall to the floor with a thunderous crash as the man sweeps his fleshy arm across the shelves of an old oaken bookcase. His rage swelling by the moment, the man picks up one ancient volume and hurls it straight at the television set. Bellowing powerful curses that would cause a demon to shrink in dismay, he pays no attention as the book reduces the unlucky screen to twisted wires hanging amid smoked glass shards.

"Devil-blasted sodomites will be here any minute!" he growls at an alchohol-soaked fetus sitting in a jar on an untouched wooden ledge as he rushes past it.

The dead homunculus offers no reply, but the obese man would not likely have noticed had it suddenly begun turning somersaults while reciting the Lord's Prayer. Bending over a black iron table marked with rusty stains that hint at its past use as a sacrificial altar, the man flips rapidly through the cracked yellow pages of an ancient book of spells. Meaty fingers run over faded spiderish writing, as his lips silently form the words of a language long since dead.

Momentarily appeased, he reaches into voluminous silk robes to find a black velvet bag suspended from a cord. From this he extracts six gold coins, each embossed with Oriental ideograms and with square holes punched through their centers. He tosses them en masse upon the table with a flick of the wrist and studies the result, then hastily scrawls a trigram upon a loose sheet of paper. Once more he repeats the process, then returns the antique coins to their pouch and tucks them away inside his robes as he examines the completed hexagram.

Finishing his consultation, the man utters a single word, and the dry wood lying in the fireplace bursts into sudden flames. The fire burns with a greenish tint that betrays its unnatural origin. Crumpling the paper in his left hand, the sorceror turns as he tosses the wad towards the fire, failing to observe that it falls to the floor just centimeters short of its intended destination.

He lumbers into a musty, rank-smelling chamber, then turns to secure the door behind him and speaks a Word of Power to seal it magically as well. Quickly, he lights the ritual candles and bends down to chalk a rough pentagram upon the floor. Stepping into its center, he drops heavily to his knees and raises pudgy hands to the ceiling.

"Dagon! Serpent Frog! Lord of the Primal Deep and King of all that dwell within your Ocean, hear now your servant! I call you by your dread *true name and invoke your Presence here!* Akh uhll, ghol nakh ghol, akh gwarrh, D'thla-Shoggi!"

He shouts the invocation and the candle on the west side of the pentagram flickers and goes out, filling the room with an insensible feeling of tentacles and murky darkness.

The sorceror swallows hard and continues, shouting "Ereshkigal! Cthonic Mother! Queen of Death and Desert, come to your servant now! Kurnugia, evartigul, erwadahul Ninanna!"

He feels the slow approach of a dry, dusty Presence, and the murk eases somewhat as the candle to the south sputters and dies. He inhales sharply, and as he does so his parched lungs burn with the hot air of the desert. Nodding with satisfaction, he proceeds with the third step of the ritual by facing east and crying out once more.

"Mahishara! Bull-prince of demons, I summon you, in the name of the eighteen-armed one! Durga-ma ke naam se, eakdhum yahan ao!" *To the east, the candle's flame disappears instantly and a rage-filled Presence fills the room with silent howls of anger.*

The hateful power of the Rakshasa nearly penetrates the chalked shield and its binder sways on his knees before it, but manages to recover his balance. Sweating profusely now, the Darkmage closes his eyes and runs a pudgy hand across his brow before calling upon the final and most powerful link in the chain of power he is assembling. Slowly, cautiously, he turns to face the last candle burning to the north.

"Mighty King! Hear me now! Show yourself, Master of the Death Hunt! Tyruun ap ioloithas! *Come, Eternal Lord of Annuwyn!"*

Thunder booms and a wild north wind storms shrieking into the room, extinguishing the last candle as green and blue lightnings crackle explosively outside the magical boundaries of the pentagram. The fat mage's body rocks back and forth as he chants the words of his great spell, his voice unheard over the raging fury of the elemental Presences.

His working finished, the wizard bows his head and with a gesture causes the wards to fall. Greenish bolts of electricity arc over the chalked boundaries and slam into his body, hurling him to the floor in the center of the pentagram. Unconscious, he convulses like one possessed, then disappears in a flash of blinding blue light.

"Eris's Apples, he's gone!" cursed the Darkmage's treacherous apprentice, wringing his hands with dismay. "We're too late."

Dag turned towards Gorean, the shaven-headed Master of the Assembly.

"Didn't you bloody well shield me?"

The bald man shook his head ruefully as the bearded Alexi snorted with disgust.

"I set a few basic wards, but nothing that would have prevented a determined scrying from a sorceror of his power."

The Master gestured around the ransacked penthouse, watching as his fellow masters paged excitedly through rare manuals of the darkest magic while others examined mysterious paraphernalia and engaged in spirited discussions of possible applications.

"It appears he observed us and prudently took flight."

"Well, you can hardly expect him to wait around for you!" Dag laughed bitterly. "I hope you've got contacts with Unipol, because he could be anywhere. And by anywhere, I mean literally *anywhere.*"

He swore beneath his breath. "And he's sure as the Seven Hells not going to be too happy with me!"

Loremaster Alexi nodded his distinguished head in agreement with the boy's morose conclusion.

"True, but you've naught to fear. You've rendered us a service, and it's the least we can do to protect you from his wrath."

The bearded master turned and looked down his elegant nose at his superior.

"Gorean, you will provide the boy with a proper warding this time, I hope?" The bald man rolled his eyes, but before he could articulate a retort, excited shouts heralded the breaching of Tetradates' spell chamber. The two Masters dropped their dispute and rushed towards the newly opened room, leaving Dag alone to contemplate the hideous end his master was surely devising for him already.

A soft voice coughed politely behind him. "You risked much to aid us in this matter."

Dag spun around to see a slender, smooth-faced Asian of about twenty-five. His almond eyes were unreadable, but the treacherous young apprentice thought he noticed a glimmer of curiousity hidden there. Too upset to bother being polite, he replied haughtily.

"There's evil with a small e, and evil with a big E followed by a capital VIL." Dag smiled coldly. "I'm the evil with a small e, the do what thou wilt Discordian ride, you get it? But big-time EVIL, you know, soul-bargaining with devils, mass murder, and blood sacrifice, is just not my thing!"

The young Asian didn't withdraw in affronted alarm as Dag half-expected him to, but nodded thoughtfully instead.

"Yes, I think I understand." To Dag's great surprise his questioner unexpectedly grinned, then bowed deeply to him. "I am Yung Chu, and big-time evil is not my thing either!"

Dag shook his head and laughed, taking in the unadorned white robes that indicated a discipleship in the Asssembly of Logosian Order.

"No, somehow I didn't think it was."

"How perceptive. One presumes you are also very talented, to take service with one such as this Tetradates."

Dag smiled bitterly at the other's flattery, and flashed his long canines.

"What do you want, Yung Chu?"

The slender young man bowed his dark head slightly and smiled easily. He had a servile manner that made Dag's skin crawl.

"Just an answer to a simple question. Was your master in the habit of consulting the Book of Changes?"

"Yeah, he did it all the time. Why do you ask?"

"Because I believe I have found what may be a clue," Yung Chu answered humbly as he produced a wrinkled piece of paper. "Perhaps this will help us learn what has happened."

"Oh, we know what happened!" spat out an irritated voice behind them. "Though I doubt your clue will be of much use to us, Yung Chu."

The two apprentices whirled around to see an extremely disgruntled Alexi walking towards them with a worried-looking Gorean at his heels.

"The question isn't where your master went, but when!" The arrogant Loremaster was almost snarling with anger. "That fat bastard went back in time!"

Two junior officers flank the imposing figure of their commander as he strides confidently out from the confines of his staff's headquarters. As the three men reach an open field just out of sight of his army's encampment, the general sees, just as it was reported to him, the curious sight of a strangely-clad fat man lying unconscious beneath the shade of a twisted scrub tree. Sharing an amused look with one of his lieutenants, the general, himself none too slender, strolls up to the sleeping man and kicks him once, hard.

The man stirs slightly, and mutters something unintelligible, and one of the officers, following his general's example, kicks the man in the side again. The sudden pain causes the man's eyes to fly open with shock, and the bemused commander sees that the man appears to be utterly bewildered.

But as he watches, curious, the man's gaze falls upon an object lying next to him. The confusion on his fleshy face disappears, and is replaced by a crafty look of triumph. The man rises slowly to stand directly before the general, points a spread-fingered hand at the junior officers, and speaks a single word. The general is astonished to see both his staunch lieutenants slump to the ground unconscious, too surprised even to think of drawing his weapon.

Before he can react, the stranger utters a long string of harsh-sounding words. The general is horrified to see the man's face begin to melt, its features shifting as it undergoes an unnatural transformation. Thirty seconds later, he recognizes a familiar face staring at him, and in that face, death.

His frozen muscles are galvanized by terror and desperation. He leaps at the mirror image of himself, bent on its destruction, but an invisible barrier appears in front of him without warning. Blood spatters and he falls screaming to his knees, his hands cradling a shattered nose.

"Take off your clothes now or I'll boil you in your own blood!" he hears the doppelganger command in his own tongue.

The general hurries to comply, trying to ignore the waves of pain that make his head throb, imagining he can already feel his intestines heating. Minutes later the sorceror stands before him, wearing his clothes with the martial bearing of a man long accustomed to command. The general stares dully at the sorceror, his mind numb with fear, and he cannot even flinch as the evil one points a finger at him. A beam of intense green light is the last thing he sees and he collapses to the ground dead, the steamed remnants of his brain smoking from his eyes, ears, and nostrils.

Pausing only to retrieve a book lying upon the barren ground, the disguised wizard walks towards his waiting army, followed by the two lieutenants, revived from their slumber, who stumble slowly after him in a dream-like state of trance. The corpse of the dead general lies lifeless beneath the naked rays of a merciless sun, steam still spiraling upwards from its ruined face.

The two young magic-users sat next to one another near the back of the formal council room. Due to the gravity of the situation, over forty of the Assembly's most powerful adepts had been assembled at short notice, and there were even a few ebon-colored robes sprinkled in amidst the predominantly red- and white-clad crowd. Not wishing to draw attention to himself, Dag had borrowed clothing from Yung Chu, and together they listened closely to the Order Master's concluding remarks.

"Given what we have learned from analyzing Tetradates' spell-books, in speaking with his apprentice, and from making some preliminary inquiries on the astral planes, we've determined that he has gone back in time in order to perform a ritual sacrifice that he could not easily arrange at this moment."

Gorean looked tired, Dag thought, no doubt the bald old man had performed many of the astral projections himself.

He wondered idly if the Assemby had considered contacting any of the leading denizens of the Sixth Hell. Maltyrakh and Svarozjic, the archdemon's ducal rivals, would certainly be forthcoming with any information that might hinder their hated adversary, but they were just as surely unaware of Ravana's unholy arrangement with Dag's former master.

The crowd buzzed and tittered in response to a statement from Master Gorean, and Dag returned his attention to the podium, wondering what he had just missed.

"What did he say?" he asked Yung Chu.

"Shhh!" was the young Asian's response.

"...that is to say, he could of course easily arrange to have the requisite number of people killed, but apparently not in a manner that would satisfy the ritual element involved. Murdering great quantities of human beings is, sadly, nothing remarkable in this day and age, but for whatever reason, bombs and other means of mass destruction have not been deemed acceptable to the Lords of the Hells. For ritual purposes, that is," the Master added hastily.

A few white-robed adepts shouted questions at the podium, but Gorean shook his bald head and held out a hand imploringly to the crowd.

"If you seek more information on these matters, please don't ask me, I'm simply repeating what I've been told by my esteemed colleagues here." He politely indicated three elderly black-robed men sitting in the front row.

"Now we have concluded that the Darkmage has gone back to a historical period where millions of people have perished in such a way that will satisfy his end of his compact with the archdemon. Judging from our admittedly limited information on the current political situation in the Sixth Hell, this great sacrifice will likely endow Ravana with the power he requires to vanquish his opponents and consolidate his grip there, possibly with an eventual challenge to one of the ranking Archdevils in mind.

"The effects of such a challenge upon our world would likely be profound, if indirect. Though we of the Logos naturally oppose all Nether Powers on principle, we are at least familiar to a certain extent with the minds and methods of Abraxas, Asmodai, Belial, and the like. Duke Ravana is a hitherto unknown factor, and were he to come to a throne on the Seventh or Eighth Hell, we have reason to believe that he would pursue a far more aggressive policy than any of the current ruling Dukes. Therefore, we must work to ensure that this does not happen!"

The Master paused for a moment, glancing about the room with a steely-eyed gaze, then continued solemnly.

"We do not know what Tetradates himself has to gain from this, but we can assume that since he is evil, intelligent, and self-centered in the extreme, it must be something substantial. The possibility of this Darkmage returning to our time, with his power and prestige enhanced by an unholy ally from the Nether Realms, is a very real one. In fact, it is my contention that Tetradates has demonstrated himself to be an immediate cause for concern to this Assembly!"

In emphasis, he smashed his fist down upon the wood of the podium in front of him.

"Therefore, I am determined to hunt him down immediately." Gorean's voice grew strong and cold, forcefully reminding the Assembly they were neither powerless nor weak. "I will send back three of our most skilled Adepts, to the times and places we have deemed to be of maximum interest to the Darkmage. Their mission is to prevent Tetradates from carrying out this blasphemy, by any means necessary!"

The Master raised his right hand in an aggressive summons.

"Shail Nagaruna, Derek Utberg, and Charles DeWitt, stand, if you will!"

His strong voice carried clearly through the crowded room. The seated magic-users whispered loudly amongst themselves as three men rose slowly to their feet, two clad in white, one in red.

"Will you accept this charge, by the Anchor and the Tree?" he demanded of them.

One after another, each of the three adepts indicated his acceptance and sat down.

"Thank you," Master Gorean nodded gratefully to the three adepts. "Tonight, at midnight, the time-traveling spell will be cast by Khul-Hazal, who will be supervised by myself, the Lore Master, and three ranking Adepts," he emphasized, quickly stifling the inevitable murmurs of dissent at the participation of a Discordian mage. "Our emissaries will attempt to stop Tetradates with a minimal amount of historical interference.

"Adept Utberg will be sent back to 1933, to investigate the Nazi era in Western Europe. Since this is the most obvious choice, I consider it to be unlikely that Tetradates will be there." The bald man shrugged. "Nevertheless, it's best to be sure."

"Adept DeWitt will travel to the year 1347, the time of the most serious outbreak of the Black Death in Europe. This is unlikely, but it is theoretically possible that these deaths would satisfy Tetradates' presumed requirements, and again, I think it best to play it safe. Finally, Adept Nagarjuna will return to the year 720 BC, to the time of the expansion of the Assyrian empire under Sargon II. Clues we have found as well as information from our astral inquiries lead us to believe that this is the era that Tetradates has chosen. We wish all three men the best of luck and…"

"Just a moment!" a voice called from the audience. "What about the Ukrainian famine engineered by the Stalin regime of the 1950's?"

The Master of the Assembly nodded his head and responded readily.

"A good question. We considered the possibility of the infamous Great Leap Forward as well. But I am told that death by starvation, even by design, is not deemed an acceptable sacrifice, perhaps since neither blood nor fire is directly involved. Are there any further questions?"

When no one else spoke up he raised a slim hand in dismissal. "Enough has been said. May the Logos aid us all in this matter."

Yung Chu followed Dag out of the hall quietly, too lost in thought to take part in the lively discussions that were breaking out in the crowded Council hall. He noticed a troubled look on his companion's angular face.

"What's the matter?"

Dag shook his head. "I'm not sure. I have to go and think about something."

He looked down at the shorter Asian and his blonde-lashed eyes narrowed.

"Are you free tonight, around ten o'clock?"

Yung Chu nodded his assent.

"Good," Dag replied. "I'll find you in your chambers then."

Yung Chu nodded again and watched as the Discordian walked quickly towards the eastern exit, his borrowed white robes trailing behind him.

"So, what are you thinking?" Yung Chu asked a few hours later, as he watched Dag trace a complicated pattern on a blank piece of paper.

Incense trailed upwards toward the ceiling, filling the small room with sweet smoke as the evil apprentice completed the ideograph and turned towards him. They were both dressed less formally than before, in t-shirts and jeans.

"I think I know where Tetradates is."

"Which is…" Yung Chu prompted him.

"Not where the Assembly thinks he is." Dag rubbed at his scars. "Do you remember the hexagram you found at the apartment?"

"Yes, of course. Number thirty-five, Chin."

"And the reading was?"

Yung Chu closed his eyes, trying to picture the crumpled piece of paper in his mind. Then the image returned to him, and he was able to state the quote with confidence.

"For the top. 'He advances as with lowered horns, intent solely upon subduing the cities. Whether his affairs go awry or prosper, he is not in error, but for him to persist thus would involve him in ignominy.'"

He grinned at Dag. "I suppose killing thirty million people could be construed as ignominious."

Dag nodded his head in silent agreement.

"So why not Sargon II, then?" Yung Chu asked.

"Too obvious," Dag replied. "Your Master Gorean and the Assembly are acting on the incorrect assumption that history is immutable."

He bit his upper lip as he handed Yung Chu the paper on which he'd been drawing.

"What do you make of this?"

Yung Chu studied the hexagram carefully.

"Double K'un is K'un of course. Hmmm…" He glanced up at Dag and shrugged. "I don't recall. What does the text say?"

Dag flipped open a slim leather-bound book and read out loud.

"Passive principle, sublime success! Its omen is a mare. The Superior Man has an objective and sets forth to gain it. At first he goes astray, but later finds his bearings. It is advantageous to gain friends in the West and South, but friends in the East and North will be lost."

He closed the book with an audible snap and cocked a pale eyebrow.

"Now use your imagination."

Yung Chu pursed his lips in thought.

"Let's see. I imagine your inquiry concerned where Tetradates disappeared to, right?"

Dag nodded affirmatively, but did not speak.

"Then, hmmm… There's a horse culture of sorts involved, obviously, and a great man, presumably a historical figure of note. West and south is good, but east and north…"

Dag nodded again.

"Never mind that for now. Where is he?" He stared into Yung Chu's dark eyes, seeking an answer. "Where is he? Don't resort to logic, don't try to think it through, just let your mind flow freely. What does it tell you, Yung Chu?"

Yung Chu swallowed and replied as the obvious answer appeared like magic in his head.

"Twelve hundreds. Mongolian empire. Temujin. It's got to be Temujin."

Dag leaned back and smiled approvingly at the young white-robe's quick understanding.

"Exactly! The Khan of Khans. Genghis. That's just what I came up with myself."

Yung Chu shook his head, exhaling to release his psychic tension as Dag rose gracefully to his feet and opened a thick black book lying on the oak desk to a page that had been marked.

"Now take a look at this," Dag told him.

Yung Chu walked over to the desk and bent over the book.

" 'Subutai had swiftly grown to enormous stature and bulk; none of the steppe horses could carry him far, and he customarily traveled in an iron wagon...' " he read aloud.

The Logosian acolyte looked up from the book with a puzzled look on his face.

"What is this? Subutai was one of Genghis Khan's four Hounds, not a fat man on a cart!"

"Think again, Yung Chu," Dag grinned knowingly. "Look at the cover."

Yung Chu did as he was told.

"The Secret History of the Mongols," he said, correctly interpreting the ideograms. "I know I've read this before and I'm almost positive it didn't say anything like that!"

"I doubt it did. But what if history itself is changing even as we speak?" Dag indicated the book. "I know Tetradates cast a time-link spell on certain books, keeping them up to date as the historical events recorded within them changed. This is one of them. Interesting, too, that he chose this particular book."

Yung Chu ignored his musings, still too unsettled by the shocking implications of the altered text.

"But you're saying that history isn't static, but fluid!"

"Well, dynamic at any rate."

"Why don't I know about this?" Yung Chu was horrified. He could not have been more alarmed if an abyss had suddenly opened up under his feet. "Do the Masters know?"

"I should think they must, but I suppose the knowledge is most likely suppressed."

"Why?"

Dag sighed and shook his head.

"Because your Assembly couldn't accept this, they'd be too afraid of the possibilities."

His hands described a circle as he attempted to make his new friend understand.

"If the past can be altered through magic, then magic becomes an intrinsically destabilizing element in what is a much more chaotic reality than is commonly imagined. Your Masters believe their magic serves the cause of a positivist Order in a rational universe, so the idea of a dynamic history looks heretical, if not downright evil to them."

Yung Chu was uncertain.

"I don't think that's necessarily so... I mean, if our cause is Order, then surely the possibility of a Discordian tampering with the past is simply an example of the very importance of our duty." His slim eyebrows raised in speculation. "Maybe this is why we have been given our power."

"Whatever gets you through the night. Look, the theological implications are not a concern of mine, okay?" Dag pointed towards the door. "Go tell them yourself. I'll be here when you need me."

An hour later, a furious Yung Chu stalked back into the room, muttering angrily under his breath. Dag's eyes danced with amusement but he pretended not to hear the Logosian's near-blasphemous imprecations. For a long moment the slim Asian stood before the window, arms folded, staring silently out at the courtyard below. Finally he turned to speak.

"They didn't listen. You knew they wouldn't!" he spat accusingly.

Dag nodded, but did not reply.

"Fools, all of them! Even Master Gorean! And Alexi..."

The junior Adept's voice trailed off, but Dag suspected he knew where the greater part of Yung Chu's fury was directed. Dag let him stew in silence for another few minutes, then rose from the desk where he'd been reading.

"Then we'll take matters into our own hands." He pointed to the book upon the desk as he started to leave. "Why don't you read up on where we're going, and I'll go finish a few preparations I want to make. I'll be back in an hour, two at most."

Yung Chu looked alarmed.

"But you can't cast a spell of that nature here! They'll feel the astral disturbance and interrupt before we can finish!"

"No they won't. They'll be too busy, I'll bet. Friends in the North, remember!" He paused in the doorway. "And, Yung Chu?"

"Yes?"

"If anyone asks about me, you don't know where I am."

"But we can't–" Yung Chu tried to protest, but before he could finish his sentence, the sorcerer's apprentice drew the door quietly shut, and disappeared.

Derek Utberg sits quietly in the maximum-security council room, blond hair and Aryan profile accented dramatically by the black-and-silver uniform of a ranking SS general. A top aide to Fieldmarshal Rommel presents to the Fuhrer the latest information on the situation in Northern Africa, but the adept pays him no attention.

Instead he focuses his astral self outward, searching for signs of magical tampering with any of the twenty or so men in the room. He delves quickly into the minds of a Wehrmacht general and a heavyset air marshal, both to no avail, then recoils upon coming into contact with the twisted obscenities that writhe inside the head of a fellow Gestapo officer. The knowledge that the man's warped mind does not stem from an outside source is of little comfort, and it is with some relief that Utberg turns his focus towards the next man, a civilian party official.

He is too caught up in his investigations to note the end of the major's presentation and does not realize that another has detected the astral disturbances created by his scans. Adolf Hitler, the Leader of his adopted country and an accomplished tantric sorcerer, observes with surprise a faint purple aura emanating from the head of one of his generals.

A closer look reveals nothing but psychic shields tightly drawn about the general's closed mind. Caught up in their surreptitious activities, neither adept notices the rapid exit of Rommel's aide, nor realizes the significance of a briefcase left behind under the large wooden table. Abandoning his fruitless examinations, the spy from the future returns his attention to the table's head and is shocked to discover the rabid eyes of the Austrian boring deeply into his own. His awareness dims momentarily as an invisible fist cruelly grasps his mind, attempting to crush his psychic wards. He stifles a cry and achieves a temporary respite as a reflexive thrust at the mind of the other causes the iron grip to relax for a second.

But only for a second, for the invisible fist returns like lightning, smashing into his mind as his mental shields disintegrate. Desperately, he lashes out with a bolt of raw power, only to see it deflected harmlessly beneath the table. He sinks in despair as his last defenses are penetrated, laying his secret thoughts open to his adversary.

Under the table, the forgotten briefcase falls to its side, absorbing full force of the magical blast. Derek Utberg finds sudden release in the void as the bomb concealed inside it explodes prematurely, killing him instantly and freeing his violated mind.

A few moments later, his wounded adversary regains consciousness. Before the clamoring officers outside manage to enter, the bleeding Austrian crawls painfully over to the adept's bomb-blasted body, and carefully removes an unusual ruby pendant from around the corpse's neck.

"Did you have anything to do with this?" Yung Chu asked quietly.

Dag only shook his head, too busy with his preparations to speak.

In the hall outside the quiet candle-lit room the Asian apprentice could hear worried voices and the hurried rush of sandle-clad feet. They were alone inside a tiny library located two stories underground in the great Assembly building, constructed centuries before to commemorate a learned Loremaster now condemned to obscurity.

He scanned the rows of books bound in decaying leather, desperately trying to turn his mind from the dark suspicions he was beginning to harbor of his companion. He returned one slim manual back to its proper place and turned to face Tetradates' apprentice. Former apprentice, he reminded himself. Former apprentice.

The sight before him did little to allay his fears. The Discordian was kneeling before an opened spellbook, whispering harshly in a tongue the Order adept knew but would never dare to speak. Blood dripped from an opened vein in his wrist into a bowl carved of white bone, and Yung Chu tried not to think on its origins as he stared at the thick red fluid pooling there.

He started as Dag grunted with satisfaction and began to bind up his wrist with a clean white cloth. The Scandinavian youth smiled at him cynically and beckoned him forward.

"Is that a chirul crystal you're wearing around your neck?"

Yung Chu nodded.

The Discordian grimaced and shook his head. "Has it occurred to you that the spell I'll be casting is a Discordian spell, after all?"

"Of course! Why…" Yung Chu's voice trailed off and he dropped his eyes to the floor. "I didn't think of that," he admitted sheepishly.

"It's okay. You can still bring it with you. It won't interfere with anything as long as you're not actually wearing it."

The blond youth laughed briefly, and Yung Chu saw dark amusement momentarily brighten his companion's cold eyes.

"It might come in handy, now that I think about it. I'll probably be wishing I could wear one myself if we run into my master."

The Discordian absent-mindedly scratched at his scarred face, then returned to his preparations.

"You might want to close your eyes about now. You might not find the presence of some of our arriving guests terribly… comfortable."

Yung Chu nodded and removed the blue crystal from around his neck and held it clenched in a white-knuckled hand.

"I don't want to know any more," he shuddered. "Just do what you have to do!"

He closed his eyes and dropped to his knees, hearing the soft scratch of the chalk against the hardwood floor as Dag sketched a protective magick circle. He willed his mind to trance, ignoring the deep sacrilege being performed around him by focusing on the blessed writings of the Great Ox.

'But evil is not known by Order through itself, otherwise evil would be in Order; for the thing known must be in the knower.'

"Ghul nakh ghul! Akh gwarrh…"

'Therefore, if evil is known through something else, namely, through good, it will be known by It imperfectly; which cannot be, for the knowledge of Order is not imperfect.'

"Eakdhum yahan ao!"

'Therefore Order does not know evil things!'

The green lightning roared as the magic shield was dropped and the young white-robe's mind found solace in unconsciousness as he collapsed beside the Discordian. The unearthly bolts hissed and crackled around their jerking bodies for a short moment, then blue light flared and they were gone.

"Where are we going, Dag?" Yung Chu whispered as they crouched outside the walls of the royal palace of the Emperor. "Is Tetradates somewhere out there?"

He pointed towards the red glow of the torch-lit outer walls. Peking was surrounded by the horse-archers of the great barbarian Khan; the city had been besieged for months but was still unvanquished. Beyond the lighted towers of sun-dried brick lay the great goat-skinned tents of Temujin, and somewhere within those tents lurked the evil mind of the Darkmage Tetradates.

"We're going to find someone important," Dag replied quietly. "The city will fall at dawn."

"How do you know that? You can't possibly know that!"

"Of course I can!" Dag patted the padlocked book at his side. "I looked it up once we got here. The link spell held. Listen!"

"Acting under the advice of his general Subutai, the Khan ordered that the Yangtze be diverted, thus depriving the city of its water supply," he read out loud to Yung Chu.

"See, when the Khitan nobles realized this they opened the city gates to the Mongols, but only after giving the Golden Emperor time to escape to Kai-Feng in the south."

Dag pointed to the palace looming over their heads.

"The Emperor departed at nightfall, so that means the gates will be opened in a few hours. I'll bet you anything that Subutai is really my old master by now. I know how the fat bastard thinks, and since Subutai is Temujin's man, that's who he'll replace."

"But if tonight's the night, we'll be massacred along with the rest!" Yung Chu was aghast at the prospect, and he couldn't understand how his companion could be so composed.

Dag shook his head and smiled reassuringly.

"We'll be fine. Trust me. But first we have to find a certain scholarly gentleman." He rose to his feet and smoothed his stolen thirteenth century Chinese garb. "Let's go."

A few hours and a number of attention-diverting spells later, the two young magic-users stood in an ornately decorated hallway in the east wing of the palace. A pale glow around the edges of an intricately carved wooden door indicated that the occupant of the small chamber was still awake and at his duties.

Yung Chu reached out to knock, but Dag, sensing someone approaching them from the far end of the hallway, grabbed his arm and pulled him back roughly behind the cover of a huge silken tapestry on the southern wall. They heard the soft footsteps of two or three men, leather-shod for silence. Yung Chu could see very little through the tapestry, but the metallic clank of swords being drawn from scabbards was unmistakable, as the shadowy figures paused for a moment before the doorway.

Then the armed men burst violently through the unlocked door, and Yung Chu cringed as he heard the sound of iron slicing through flesh and bone, and the meaty thud of a body hitting the floor. Then there was only silence as the assassins padded softly out the door and retreated down the hall in the direction from which they had first appeared.

Dag slipped from behind the tapestry, and after looking down the hallway to make sure the killers had no intention of returning, beckoned for Yung Chu to join him. Reluctantly, the Logosian apprentice crept out from his hiding place and followed his companion into the room of the dead scholar.

He fought the gorge that threatened to rise from his stomach as he forced himself to look at the murdered man. The victim was young, about his own age, and of a similar build. His clothes were rich, yet simple, and his face was finely formed with the sensitivity one might expect in a scholar, or a priest. One blade had gutted his stomach, while another had swept down across his body, crushing his collarbone and nearly severing his head.

"Good!" Dag commented coolly. "The one thing I feared was that they'd take his head. That would've been a problem!"

Yung Chu could only stare at the Discordian apprentice, too appalled to speak. The horror, the nausea, was almost too much to bear. "His head?" he finally managed to ask.

"Yeah, we needed to know what he looked like." Dag smirked at him. "You're going to take his place after all, and we needed to be sure he didn't have any distinguishing features like a scar or a missing tooth. All those earlier visitors did was save me the trouble of killing him myself."

Yung Chu chose to ignore the frightful implications of that statement, and focused on the assassins instead.

"Who killed him? And why?"

"I assume Tetradates had him killed. His name is Yeh Che'lyu Tsai, and after being captured by Mongol soldiers during the fall of Peking, he was taken to the Khan. He was Khitan, but his loyalty to his Chinese overlords pleased Temujin to the point that he was made chief astrologer to the Khanate. He was in a position to influence the Khan against his more bloodthirsty generals. Like Subutai."

Dag laughed gleefully, his long hair flying free as his ill-fitting wide-rimmed hat fell off.

"Tetradates is going to freak when you show up instead of the unfortunate Mr. Tsai tomorrow!"

"But what about you?"

"What about me? I can't stay with you, you know. I'm not Asian, and Tetradates would strip a shapemasking glamor in a second. Nobody in the Khan's court knows what Yeh Che'lyu Tsai looked like, so you'll pass without a problem."

"But... but where are you going? Back to our time? You can't leave me here!"

"Of course not. I'll ride to Austria and raise the defenses against the possibility of a European expedition. There's a certain princeling thereabouts who reportedly had long blond hair."

The Discordian's eyes glittered dangerously.

"You mean you're going to kill him!" Yung Chu blurted out, terrified of this ruthless aspect of his companion's character.

Dag shook his head patiently and tried to mollify him.

"Do you have a better idea? Look, do you really think I can just ride up to the Most Holy Roman Emperor and tell him 'Hi, I'm from the future and I'd like to borrow your armies in case the little yellow people come?'" He chuckled indulgently. "Come on, Yung Chu, don't be such an idiot. Sometimes people have to die so that more people won't."

He bent his tall frame over and carefully slung the corpse of the Chinese scholar over his right shoulder.

"Now I'll get rid of the body and you clean up this mess on the floor. Just change into one of his robes, fix your hair into a topknot, and wait to get captured. Don't forget to impress the Khan! I'll contact you from Europe; we can firetalk without too much trouble. In the meantime, just do whatever you can to counter anything Tetradates is telling the Khan."

Yung Chu only stared as the young Discordian mage grunted as he rose unsteadily to his feet and walked carefully out the door, blood still dripping from the lifeless burden. The Logosian closed his eyes and listened until the heavy footsteps were gone, leaving him alone in the past, trapped inside a besieged city doomed to fall in only hours. He lay back on the dead scholar's bed and wept, tears of fear, guilt, and shame wetly streaking his cheeks.

"What do you mean, we won't go after them?" snarled Alexi. "Have you lost your mind!"

The angry Loremaster's voice shook with fury as he glared at the cool grey eyes of his superior.

The Master of Order calmly shook his shaven head and grimaced wearily at the Loremaster's insubordination.

"No, Alexi, I have not lost my mind. But you, I'm afraid, have lost your temper!"

A note of steel entered his voice as he pointed a finger at the bearded man.

"It is unseemly and if you would speak further, I will hear a civil tongue! Is that clear?" His iron tone brooked no challenge, and the Loremaster bowed his head in submission.

"Yes, I… I must apologize. It is only… it is my utmost concern that we stop this evil sorceror from consumating his blasphemous plans."

"I understand and share your concerns–" the Master of Order started to say, but Alexi interrupted him.

"Then why do we wait here, useless? The apprentices have located the evil one, so let us move to end this madness." The exasperated master threw his hands up towards the ceiling. "I beg you, send me, or Cummings, or one of the Jains, or even go yourself! But we must stop Tetradates and we cannot do it from here!"

He stared at the Master of Order, his fists clenched on his hips.

The Master placed his hands together in the shape of a temple, and stroked his chin contemplatively. He cleared his throat and his eyes narrowed as he regarded the other.

"You realize we have already lost two Adepts, two of our best."

"Of course. Utberg and DeWitt. What of it?"

"And you think these deaths were mere accident?" The Master's left eyebrow rose skeptically and for a moment the Loremaster looked uncertain.

"Well, we did not know that Hitler was a sorcerer of such strength. As for the plague era, well, millions of people did die of the disease after all, it was just misfortune that the vaccine failed."

"Really?" The Master's voice was dry. "And it was just happenstance as well that Tetradates' own apprentice should choose this particular time to betray him, so close to the moment of his master's greatest triumph? I wonder, Alexi, I really do. There appear to be wheels within wheels here, and I am sorely afraid I have been deceived!"

It was a painful admission. The deaths of two, perhaps even three good men were already on his conscience. He was loathe to add any more to that score.

"But that's impossible!" the Loremaster protested. "I essayed Truthscan on Tetradates' apprentice myself!"

"As did I, my friend. But we do not truly know the depths of the darker Discordian magicks, and it may well be that a cunning Darkmage like Tetradates has ways of hiding secrets within a willing mind. I have wondered much since the two boys disappeared so suddenly, and I dread to think of what may have happened to young Yung Chu."

The Loremaster nodded grimly in agreement.

"Every night I pray for his safekeeping. But surely if he is endangered by the dark apprentice, that is all the more reason why we must pursue them now, is it not?"

"No." The Master of Order shook his head. "The communication I received was from the Discordian, not Yung Chu. Although he claims they have located the Darkmage, and that Yung Chu is well, I fear he may be lying. No Alexi, I will not risk another of the Assembly, not just yet."

"Then what shall we do?" The Loremaster's eyes, for once, were not the least bit arrogant. They were dark and haunted with fear.

"We wait, old friend. We wait and we pray."

Yung Chu grimaced as he pulled the evil-smelling coverings closer to him, trying to ward off the chill of the northern Chinese night. The rancid goatskins were malodorous and rough to the touch, and he thought longingly of the fine silks that had adorned Yeh Che'lyu's chambers, wishing he had thought to bring them with him at the time of his capture.

Outside his tent, he heard drunken shouts and the terrified screams of women captured at the fall of Peking, now condemned to live out the rest of their short lives as barbarian playthings. His position as Chief Astrologer had assured his own survival and his newfound status allowed him a certain degree of privacy, but his modern conscience made it impossible for him to ignore some of the indecencies of conquest's aftermath.

He groaned as yet another woman screamed piercingly, her long despairing cry cut short by a guttural oath and the sharp crack of an open-handed blow. Then there was silence, almost, as the woman's quiet sobs were drowned out by a sudden gust of wind from the north. The tent rattled and shook, but held firm and Yung Chu rolled over on his side in a futile search for sleep. It had been a long night.

Just as the first rays of dawn were appearing in the east, a hand grasped his shoulder and shook him awake. Yung Chu started momentarily at the man's rough Mongolian speech and then relaxed as he remembered where he was. And, he reminded himself, who he was supposed to be.

"You are to attend the Khan at his council, immediately!" the soldier ordered.

His soft leathers and fine Chinese sword marked him as one of the Khan's personal bodyguards, his presence a testimonial to the high regard in which the Khan held his Astrologer. Not a bad omen, thought Yung Chu.

He rubbed the sleep from his eyes and glared at the bodyguard's pockmarked face. "Where is it being held?" he asked, replying in the barbarian tongue.

"The Great Yurt, of course."

"Very well." He stood and looked down his nose at the shorter Mongol. "You will wait outside while I make my preparations. Then you will escort me to the council!"

He gestured his dismissal and the Khan's bodyguard, taken aback at his firmness, bowed deeply.

"Yes sir! I am at your command."

A few minutes later he strode confidently into the Khan's goatskin tent. It was huge, large enough for the ruler of many lands and diverse peoples to hold court in. Now it was half empty, with only a score of servants and pleasure girls wandering about inside the interior, oblivious to the warlike men clustered around a large man seated on a cluster of pillows towards the back of the tent.

As Yung Chu drew closer, the warriors nearest him began to step out of his way. The movement attracted the seated man's attention, and Temujin looked up, glaring at the intruder. But the irritated look disappeared instantly and the Khan's broad face creased into a smile as he recognized the Khitan councillor.

"Ahhh, Yeh Che'lyu, I am glad to see you!"

The strangely golden eyes that looked so like a cat's were gleaming. Yung Chu wondered what had caused the Khan to be in such good humor, but quickly put the thought aside. He'd find out soon enough.

"I exist only to serve you, Great Khan! May this unworthy servant be ever at your command, Great One."

Yung Chu swept low in a formal courtly bow and Temujin beamed. It was interesting to see how these bloodthirsty barbarians fervently admired the civilized manners and flowery words of the ancient culture they had so ruthlessly conquered.

As he rose from his obeisance, the young Asian's gaze swept across the generals standing behind their seated ruler. He marked Mukali and Bogurchi, Jebei the Arrow, Juchi, the Khan's half-Merkit son, and Chagatai, the heir apparent. He noted Jelme, other than himself, the only non-Mongol, a forest dweller who had once saved Temujin's life and now ranked among the most powerful marshals of the toumans. Then his eyes met those of an imposing figure standing behind the rest, his great bulk dwarfing even that of the legendary wrestler Belgutai, who was said to have broken the back of the giant Buri Boko with his bare hands.

Yung Chu froze as he stared at the inscrutable face of the Khan's favorite general. Tetradates' shape-masking spell was perfect, for not a glimmer of Caucasian ancestry showed in the Darkmage's disguised appearance. The Logosian ventured a hesitant psychic probe and stifled a gasp as it was rebuffed by a power that dwarfed his own. Closing his eyes, he quailed and braced for the magick he feared would blast through his shields and destroy his mind. But it did not come.

"Yeh Che'lyu, what's wrong!" Yung Chu found himself embraced by a pair of strong arms as he sank to his knees waiting for a blow that never came. "Are you ill? Do evil spirits assail you?"

He unsteadily opened his eyes and found himself staring into the slitted orbs of the Great Khan.

"Father, he sees visions from the Sky!" exclaimed Temujin's middle son, Ogodai, who had caught Yung Chu from behind as he fell.

"Tell us, Yeh Che'lyu, do you see victory in the south for the toumans?"

Yung Chu's mind raced as he sought to unravel the diverse threads woven through this particular council. Temujin's good mood, Tetradates' forbearance, and now a hint from the Khan's son. He shook his head in horror as he quickly pieced the clues together and came up with a conclusion that caused his heart to grow cold. Peking was the gateway to the civilized south, and there were many cities for the sacking... and many millions of souls for the slaying. Rising to his feet, he bowed deeply again to the Khan and spoke. This was no time to mince his words, even if it cost him his life.

"I have seen... what I have seen... victory and cities falling, but in their destruction, a Sky-cursed waste. I see a foolish hubris in attempting to win that which has already been won!"

At his words, the war council broke out in a buzz of interjections and excited arguments.

"He lies to protect his former masters!"

"How could he, he wasn't here?"

"He speaks with the voice of the Sky!"

"Ha! Astrologers know nothing of war!"

But Yung Chu ignored the multitude of voices, listening only for the one that mattered most. The Great Khan stood before him, tall and broad-chested for a Mongol, a man among men. Now his square face was filled with a puzzled sadness as he surveyed his youthful Astrologer, stroking his sparse beard and shaking his pigtailed head. Yung Chu's intestines twisted as he recalled the horrific fate of those who had gainsayed Temujin before, but his beardless face remained calm and impassive.

"You would call me a fool, then, you, a man of dwindled Kara-Khitai, slaves to the Jurchet?" The Khan's voice was soft, but Yung Chu knew that danger lurked like a yawning abyss only a single step away.

He dropped to his knees and bowed his head, staring fixedly at the hide-covered floor.

"I am your slave only, Great Khan. But when a wise one seeks a mare's milk to make khouvass, does he slay the mare and drain her body dry, or does he milk her and then leave her unmolested until he once more has need for milk?"

The Khan was unmoved. For a long moment he remained silent, and Yung Chu thought he could really feel Temujin's eyes burning upon the carefully knotted hair on the back of his head. Then, as Yung Chu dared a sidelong glance, he saw the Khan's lips began to curve upward in a broad smile, and that broad, thickening belly began to shake as he roared with laughter, his amusement echoing from the goatskin walls of the giant tent.

"Fools! All of you, fools!" He spun and glared at each of his generals in turn, but saving his most scathing look for the false Subutai. "And you would have had me slay them all, short-sighted wolf! Then who would work the fields, our untamed toumans? Shall my sons turn merchant, and learn to make gold like the traders? No! Never!"

He turned back around and raised Yung Chu to his feet. "You, Astrologer. What is your advice?"

Yung Chu swallowed hard. Here was his chance. It was only a battle, not the war, but it was a victory nonetheless.

"Appoint a viceroy to rule over the Kin," he said quickly. "One who can break the remnants of their pride, but leave them free to work and trade otherwise. Tax them heavily, and use them to provide for the toumans. Your empire, Great Khan, has been conquered from the saddle. But you cannot rule it from the saddle. For that, you need a throne!"

The Khan nodded. "Wise words, Yeh Che'lyu. Mukali!" he shouted, gesturing to a tall Mongol standing off to the left of him.

"Yes, Great Khan," the man stepped forward and inclined his head respectfully.

"Mukali, you are viceroy in the south. Rule over the Kin with an iron fist, and milk them for me. Yes, milk them!" he bellowed, grinning happily at Yung Chu. The Khan's loud laughter was so infectious his generals couldn't help but join him, and even the young time-traveler had to smile.

"And you, Yung Chu, will not be just my Astrologer anymore. I have an Empire now, and I must have a Councillor worthy of an Emperor. The man who rules at the Emperor's side. What did the Kin call such a man?"

Yung Chu bowed his head, concealing his satisfaction.

"This humble servant is not worthy, Great Khan. But they called such a man... they called him Prime Minister, Majesty."

The Khan smiled.

"Then, Yeh Che'lyu Tsai, you are my Prime Minister."

Yung Chu fell to the ground and prostrated himself before the Emperor of the Steppes.

"I am always yours to command, Great One. If I speak, may it only be with your voice!"

He was pleased with himself. But as he rose to his feet to accept the many congratulations from the assembled Mongol warlords, he couldn't help but sneak a quick glance at the man whose plans he had thwarted. Tetradates betrayed no emotion, but Yung Chu knew there were demons of rage howling behind the Darkmage's disguised face. He started as a silent voice spat angry words into his mind.

You will not thwart me, Orderling. I promise you that!

That night Yung Chu fell to sleep with difficulty, and his dreams were ghastly visions of suffering and torture. Again and again, he saw himself perishing after long hours of torment at the exquisitely skilled hands of Tetradates. He saw the scaly tongues of *horgutash* demons flaying his soul from his body as skeletal bone devils snapped his limbs and sucked greedily at the marrow that slowly dripped out. Then the warning shriek of a violated warding spell jolted him awake, and he was relieved to find himself sitting upright amidst his foul-smelling skins. But he was not alone.

His black-clad assailants eyed him warily as they entered the little tent. Each man was swathed in cloth from head to toe, and bore a sharp, curved dagger. The first man, whose entry had triggered the magical alarm, also carried a short scimitar-like sword as he advanced towards Yung Chu in a crouch. Something about the man seemed familiar, the young Logosian thought as he eyed the evil-looking blade. As he backed slowly away from the men, his mind returned to another midnight assault, and that same sword dripping with the blood of a scholar.

But unlike the man he had replaced, Yung Chu was not defenseless. He smiled grimly, and cast a quick glamor over himself as he suddenly leaped to his feet.

"You thought you killed me once, fools! Do you think to try again!" he shouted angrily as he assumed one of the demonic aspects that had so recently haunted his dreams.

The three assassins quailed before the image of the *horgutash*, as it flapped its dragon-like spiked ears and drooled bloody red ichor from its gaping black maw. The hellish image was too much for two of the men, they broke and ran screaming into the night, but the man with the sword stood his ground, cringing fearfully, until Yung Chu made as if to leap at him. The sword fell to the ground, followed seconds later by its bearer as he collapsed in a dead faint.

"Oh, for Belial's sake," growled Tetradates as he strolled into the tent, still wearing the outward appearance of the dead Mongolian general. "You can't trust these superstitious primitives to do anything right!"

Yung Chu's momentary sense of victory disappeared at the sight of the Darkmage. Now it was his turn to cower as the great sorceror shrugged and extended a hand towards him.

"I suppose we'll just have to do this the old-fashioned way," Tetradates told him, before making a gesture with his left hand.

Yung Chu felt an unseen hand seem to reach inside his rib cage and grip his heart, and a sharp pain wracked his chest as the hand began to squeeze. His pectoral muscles spasmed uncontrollably and he fell to his knees, body exploding with agony. As he felt the fibers of his heart begin to tear away slowly, one by one, he clutched desperately at his breast for the chirul crystal that hung suspended there and called upon the power inside it.

He almost lost control of his bladder as the blessed crystal broke the evil magick and the pain disappeared instantly. Tetradates grunted uncomfortably, and Yung Chu looked up to see an overweight Caucasian man with a very surprised expression on his face. He crawled for the assassin's fallen sword, grasped its hilt, then leaped to his feet. With a fury inspired by fear, he raised the weapon over his head, ready to decapitate the stunned Darkmage. But like his cowardly hirelings, Tetradates had already fled into the shadows.

"What is happening, you cursed hellspawn? Where is he?"

The Loremaster's eyebrows rose as Gorean angrily addressed the scarlet riyal crystal in his hand. The crystal glowed and seemed to pulse weirdly as Dag's response echoed back over the centuries, as if keeping time with some unheard, irregular rhythm.

He's with the Khan somewhere near India. Problem is, Tetradates is there too!

"Why can't we speak with him?" Alexi interjected, leaning over the Order Master's shoulder. "How do we know you're not in league with your master?"

You don't, came the immediate reply. *And you can't speak with him because I'm in Hungary in service to Prince Henry. Yung Chu doesn't know how to use the riyal.*

"Where did you get it?" Alexi demanded.

You don't need to know. Now are you going to send someone back here or not? Yung Chu managed to keep Temujin from wiping out China, but Iran is history. My guess is that Tetradates has already got something like a third to a half of the deaths he needs to complete the pact.

"You're not serious..." Gorean blanched. "No, of course you are." He looked over at the Loremaster, who was shrugging his shoulders helplessly. "Well, Dag, I suppose we have no choice but to trust you. What would you have us do?"

Get a good team of five or six Adepts together, competent ones who are capable of taking on my master between them. Tell them not to mess around or be clever, just kill him as fast as they can. I'll contact Yung Chu tonight and find out where you should send the strike team. Have them plan to travel at the next new moon, with a group that large you won't be able to do it any sooner than that.

"Okay but wait..." The glow inside the crystal died to a dull blood-like red, and Gorean swore under his breath in frustration. "He's gone."

Yung Chu held his head in his hands as he meditated before the fire in his rudely-constructed dwelling. The last six months, he had been witness to a hell on earth, as the Khan's toumans, like the evil breath of a bloody-minded god, had swept before them the armies of the Kwaresm-shah, massacring his people and obliterating his empire. And there had been nothing Yung Chu could do to stop it.

For Temujin had not planned to war against the wealthy and powerful Muslim empire. Rather, the Great Khan had actually taken his advice to make diplomatic overtures to his counterpart across the great river of the Jaxartes. Unfortunately, the Shah Mohammed was cursed with a surfeit of pride and a dearth of good sense, and, feeling that the undisciplined horse-archers of the Mongols would melt before his fierce Islamic warriors, sent the Great Khan's ambassadors back to him with their heads shaved. Among the Mongols, this was the mark of a slave. It would have been better if the Shah had simply killed them.

The Khan was enraged, understandably, and no amount of pleading or argument would budge him from his determination to punish the Kwaresmians. Tetradates, in his guise as Subutai, designed a brilliant plan of assault, circumlocuting the Shah's armies on the banks of the Jaxartes by traversing the dangerous heights of the Pamir mountains in the cold depths of winter. The Shah was taken completely by surprise; Otrar fell first, followed by Bukhara, then Samarkand. At first, Temujin was inclined to be merciful, killing only the Kwaresmian nobles and the Turkish-manned garrisons. But as the war went on, setbacks occurred and Mongol casualties increased. The Great Khan's temper grew short. And always, there was the false Subutai, whispering in his ear.

Seventy thousand people were slain at Nissa, one million perished at Merv when the waters of the Murghab were diverted to drown the besieged city. At Herat, three thousand were spared during the first sacking of the city, but at Subutai's insistence, the toumans returned. At Nishapur, Subutai's protégé, Tului, presided over the bloodshed as every single living thing in the city was exterminated, every last man, woman, dog, cat, and rat.

And before the shattered gates of each fallen city, an immense mound of skulls was piled, a mighty tribute to the kings of death. Subutai had told Temujin that the mounds would strike fear into his enemies, that they would teach the world to quail before his armies and dread the very mention of his name. But in his ivory-and-gold mansion in the bowels of the Sixth Hell, a sated Baal-Ravana smiled and flicked his spiny tail about with anticipation.

Yung Chu had no idea of how close Tetradates was to reaching his goal. He was reeling from the magnitude of the vicious genocide, and felt only a vague sense of surprise that the Darkmage's sacrifice had not yet been completed. He had not heard from Dag since that lonely night in Peking when the Discordian had left him awaiting capture at the hands of the Mongols. Therefore he was quite startled when he heard a familiar voice whisper to him amidst the crackling of the flames.

Yung Chu, listen to me. It's Dag.

Yung Chu couldn't help a reflexive glance around the room, then, angrily, he returned his attention to the fire before him.

"Where in Chaos' name have you been? Why haven't you contacted me? Why…"

Because there hasn't been a reason to do so! Dag interrupted. *My master is more powerful than you know, and he could be listening right now. Where is he?*

"He's with Jebei besieging Tus, at the foot of the Elbuiz Mountains. It's safe to talk now, I think."

Good. What do you think he plans next?

"Well, the Khan was talking to me today about coordinating the logistics of crossing the Indus. He must be planning to invade the Punjab, I suppose. I tried to discourage him, but I think Tetradates has him under his spell. Not literally, of course, I mean, I've been keeping a close watch out for that, but I think the Khan's blood has been up ever since he destroyed the Shah. Whatever Subutai says pretty much goes nowadays."

Hmmmm. Well, regardless, you absolutely have to keep him from India. There's too many people there, and he'll finish the sacrifice in no time. Do whatever you have to, even poison the Khan if you must…

"Dag!" a shocked Yung Chu exclaimed. "I can't do that! You know we're sworn never to kill!"

Except, of course, for the occasional wizard of whom your Assembly doesn't approve, the Discordian replied drily. *Ah well, I'd hoped your time with the savages had taught you a bit more flexibility by now.*

"Besides, he named Ogodai heir now, and Ogodai practically worships Subutai." Yung Chu ignored the sarcastic rejoinder. "Killing Temujin wouldn't change much."

So poison the heir too. Look, you have to keep the armies out of India.
If you can't kill, then think of something else. But there are five Assembly
Adepts coming in less than two weeks, so if you can hold off Tetradates for
that long, we should be okay. Now I've got to go. Good luck.

"You too, Dag," Yung Chu whispered to the fire, feeling suddenly
heartsick and scared, caught out of place and time. 'You too."

His hands still coated with greasy animal fat, Yung Chu strode
rapidly to the Great Yurt, escorted by an honor guard of the Khan's
elite bodyguard. He had protested when the Khan assigned the four
men to guard him, but the rumors of a failed assassination caused
Temujin to insist upon Yung Chu's acceptance. Fearing treachery, or
a malevolent ensorcelment courtesy of Tetradates, the young disciple
of Order no longer slept without first setting an exhaustive series
of painstakingly woven wards to protect against any demonic or
metaphysical assault. Fortunately, his precautions only helped cement
his reputation among the barbarian warriors as a potent Astrologer.

Having become accustomed to their strange charge's dabbling in
the mystical arts, none of his enforced companions thought anything
of the working he had performed that morning. It wasn't a Discordian
spell, quite, but it wasn't one that his Assembly instructors would
approve of either. But since his only other altenative was quite beyond
the pale, he could only hope that the stern god of Harmony and Order
would understand his dire straits and relent when the Day of Judging
came. Putting his guilty misgivings behind him, Yung Chu entered
the Khan's goatskin tent, knowing that in only two days the nine-
tailed white banner of the Emperor of the Steppes was scheduled to
cross the Indus.

"Ah, Yeh Che'lyu! My eyes brighten with your presence," the Khan
said, openly pleased at his Prime Minister's arrival.

Kasala, the Khan's beautiful Merkit concubine, was lying at her
lord's feet but as Yung Chu drew closer to the Khan's pillowed seat, she

rose gracefully and quietly made her sinuous way towards the back of the huge tent. Yung Chu's eyes couldn't resist following the exquisite swing of her retreat, and Temujin chuckled.

"Yeh Che'lyu, your wisdom is such that I often forget how young you are. You need a wife!" At the stunned look on his Khitan minister's face, the barbarian ruler relented. "Well, at least a woman to call your own. You need one. A good woman is like a smooth-riding horse, Yeh Che'lyu; once you get in the saddle you don't want to get off!"

He sniggered lewdly and smirked as he glanced back to where the lovely Merkit girl had disappeared. "You like her? She's yours."

"The Great Khan is too kind to his miserable servant!"

Teumjin only laughed again. "You won't be miserable long!"

Once more, Yung Chu noted the Khan's unusually playful demeanor, in very much the same way that the autumn still calmed the grass just before the storm winds of the Mongolian winter began to sweep the steppes. If he had any questions about the immanency of the invasion, they were gone now.

"So why are your hands covered with fat?" the Great Khan wanted to know, pointing to Yung Chu's lard-dripping hands.

His Prime Minister bowed respectfully, extending his arms palms-up for the Khan's review.

"For you, Great Lord. I would anoint you with the Sky's blessing before your ride today." Yung Chu held his breath, awaiting the superstitious Khan's response. He felt a chill inside as Temujin arched a slender eyebrow and shook his full head of hair that was still, for the most part, as black as the ravens that fed upon the slain.

"And how did you know I planned to ride today?"

Yung Chu swallowed and took a deep breath.

"It is said that in two days the toumans begin the Indus crossing. This humble servant has noticed that the Great Khan often enjoys a ride before battle."

"Yes...heheheheh, a ride of one sort or another," the Khan joked cheerfully, slapping the younger man's shoulder. "Anoint me then, Yeh Che'lyu, for I will ride long and hard tonight!"

Letting out a slow sigh of relief, Yung Chu drew two vertical lines down the Khan's cheeks with his fingers, then connected them with a single horizontal stripe curving across the broad forehead. "Ride well, Great Lord," he said quietly. He bowed once, and departed before he could repent of his actions.

Late that night, a flash of green light exploded above the young Prime Minister's head. A man's voice shouted, more in surprise than pain, and Yung Chu heard feet pounding as he struggled to open his eyes. He muttered a few words to release the wards and sat up quickly, glancing about the tent. Shadows danced strangely in the smoky torchlight that illuminated the inside of the yurt as his nervous bodyguards kept their respectful distance. Outside the entrance, a guardsman clad in the Khan's imperial whites was clutching at his burned right hand, cursing violently, and keeping a wary eye on him.

One of his personal bodyguards bowed respectfully.

"Wise Lord, forgive us. We warned him not to wake you..."

Yung Chu brushed his apologies aside. "It's okay, Ulgunai. Is anything amiss with the Emperor?"

The Khan's man bowed even more deeply than Ulgunai. "The Khan of Khans requests your presence, Lord. He is... troubled."

Yung Chu nodded in understanding. "Go then, and tell the Khan I will attend him."

"I saw... a strange beast. Like a horse, but not a horse, standing on the banks of the Indus. Its skin was green like the spring plains, and it had a single horn, a horn like that of a goat, growing from the center of its skull. It... it spoke to me, saying 'Temujin, strong you are, but no man can battle the Sky. This passage is forbidden. Return, or death will follow!' "

The Khan's yellow face was pale, even by the crackling reddish light of the fire. "Tell me what it means," he insisted feverishly. "Yeh Che'lyu, tell me the meaning of my dream!"

"Peace, Majesty, peace… What you saw was a unicorn, one of the magical shapes that the Sky sometimes takes in the dream-world. When a man dreams, his soul leaves his body and goes to another place, where things of this world exist in different forms, and where things not of this world may appear too."

Yung Chu took a closer look at the older man's face. Clearly the spell-dream he had woven had frightened the dread ruler of the Mongols badly, even worse than he had intended. He'd forgotten just how superstitious these primitive pagans could be.

"The green color indicates sickness and disease, perhaps to be visited upon the toumans should we cross the river, or perhaps, may the Sky forbid it, to be visited upon your own person, Great Khan. But whatever the meaning, Lord, know that what is foretold in the spirit world will always come to pass."

His voice dropped lower as he strove to drive his point home.

"And the message to you is clear, Great One. Not even one warrior may ride across the river into the Punjab! The Sky forbids it!"

Genghis Khan nodded, beads of sweat dripping from his brow. "You are right, Yeh Che'lyu. We will not cross the Indus!"

The Mongol captain was in a foul mood. A week ago the invasion of the rich empire of the Punjab had been called off for reasons unknown, and he shook his head bitterly at the thought of the plump, langorous women whose embraces he would never know. He smashed a callused fist against the worn leather of his saddle, infuriated by the knowledge that the wealthy, unwalled cities of the lower Indus valley remained safe and inviolate in their innocent splendor.

The knowledge that the Tanguts of Hsi Hsia had revolted again against their Mongol overlords gave him little cheer despite the

promise of a good fight sure to be offered by the proud eastern
tribes. It was going to be a long, cold winter, and the captain had
been looking forward to spending it in the sensual surroundings of
a fallen Punjabi city, not warring against a familiar enemy on the
frozen steppes. The captain scowled as one of his lieutenants rode
up alongside him, and he glowered at the sallow-skinned young man
as he made his report. He paid little heed as the lieutenant droned
on and on, until the mention of an unusual party traveling south
captured his attention.

"...and Gogido said they did not even try to hide or run away!"
The young man paused and reflected a moment. "Perhaps they are
spies?"

The captain's narrow eyes almost disappeared as he squinted at the
horizon. "It is a strange thing," he mused aloud. "Five men, dressed
as Kin peasants, traveling far from their homeland. And taking little
note of our patrols···I do not like that!"

Thoughtfully, he chewed at his lower lip, reflecting on the possibilities as his horse continued its easy canter north. At last, he reached a
decision.

"They cannot be peasants. If they are not merchants attempting to
avoid our taxes, they must be Tangut spies. Either way, we will take
no chances. Take a troop of archers and ambush them as they crest a
hilltop. Bring me their heads."

An hour later, hearing the sound of onrushing hooves, the captain
looked up and saw the young lieutenant galloping excitedly towards
him, holding a heavy sheepskin bag slung before him.

"You were wise, lord, to take precautions!" the lieutenant exclaimed. "For as they reached the top of the hill, we greeted them
with a hailstorm of arrows, and the Sky guided our shafts! Look!"

He lifted the bag from his horse's back and disgorged its contents
upon the ground. Five severed heads lay there, still oozing blood and
ichor. Three were Kin, but one appeared to be burned to a black crisp
by the sun. And the last was hairless, its skin a strange pink color

similar to that of the red-haired slaves the captain had seen once in the conquered cities of Khorasan.

"A demon, then," he grunted, nodding approvingly at the lieutenant. "Well done!"

The Mongol cavalry rode on towards the great army assembling in Balkash. Behind them the sightless green eyes of the Master of Order stared fixedly at the endless horizon of the Transoxian plain.

"Where are they!" Yung Chu whispered urgently into the fire. He wanted to release his anxieties by screaming at it, but didn't dare for fear of waking Kasala. Although like his bodyguards she had started to become used to his strange customs, he had no doubts that shrieking at nothing but burning kindling would manage to terrify the sleeping beauty. "You said they'd be here a week ago!"

They should have arrived by now, Dag responded. The Discordian sounded worried. *Has Tetradates been out of the camp?*

"No, he and the other generals have been closeted with the Khan for the past ten days. The Tanguts are proving a harder nut to crack this time around, and Temujin's recalled all of our top strategists from the field. I think they're trying to come up with a new plan of attack."

Well, that's good. Where in Eris's name can they be? Did you just say, our? You're starting to think like a Mongol!

Yung Chu snorted, and they both fell silent for a minute or two, until a dark thought occurred to Yung Chu.

"Dag, remember the reading?" he asked. "The one that led us here in the first place?"

Yeah, of course. Why... oh, devils! the Discordian exclaimed. *That's not good.*

"No, I don't think so. The only question is, are they the friends in the East or the North?"

Cursed if I know. The voice inside the crackling flames fell quiet again, but Yung Chu knew the irritable Discordian was swearing under his breath. *Looks like I'll have to contact the Assembly again and see what's taking them. In the meantime, take advantage of any opportunity to… you know, shake things up in the camp.*

"Perhaps," Yung Chu said wearily. "I'll see what I can do."

Dag's sigh was audible. *All right. Well, the Tanguts don't have any cities worth speaking of so I doubt Tetradates will bother there, which should buy us the time we need. Sit tight, and I'll keep you posted. Adios!*

The flames rose momentarily with a greenish flare then settled down and continued to lick hungrily at the firewood. Yung Chu sat and stared at the glowing reds and golds of the fire, silently wrestling with his conscience as he listened to the hissing and popping sounds of the wood being devoured.

"Who were you talking to, Yeh Che'lyu?" he heard a sultry voice behind him murmur.

Unsettled, he spun around on his buttocks to see Kasala's almond eyes staring at him. She blinked once and licked painted lips with her dainty tongue, carefully studying his face. Though he doubted the Khan had ordered her to spy on him, he was loathe to put anything past the wily Mongol ruler.

"Only a fire demon, lovely one," he lied easily. "His name is Sivarodai and he roams the hells like a wolf upon the steppes, preying on the damned souls there."

He was amused to see her eyes widen as a look of alarm crossed her lovely face. Her fear almost made him burst out laughing.

"Now I must go and tell the Khan of the evil secrets he has whispered to me."

"But it is late to call upon the Great One!" the captured courtesan protested.

Yung Chu slowly stood up and surveyed the kneeling woman, her splendid golden body covered meagerly by the captured Turkish bedsilks, her high breasts quivering only slightly as she strove to hide her fear of him. The young apprentice licked his lips as a warm heat began to rise below his belly.

"Perhaps you are right, it is late, yes!"

He smiled in anticipation and took her slender hand in his own. He had broken so many of his vows already. What was one more?

As the cool night breeze froze the glistening sweat into miniscule salt crystals upon his body, Yung Chu walked noiselessly across the Mongol camp to the Khan's great tent. He passed several bodyguards, but the keen-eyed warriors in white never saw him, not even when he ducked his head and slipped through the entrance. He was invisible thanks to the masking spell he'd cast after Kasala had drifted safely off to sleep.

Two hours after midnight, most of the tent's inhabitants were sleeping also, although soft cries and grunting noises betrayed the activities of a few tireless couples. Stealthily, Yung Chu made his way towards the Khan's usual place at the back, tip-toeing around the slumbering bodies of two pretty young Kin slave girls and a fat, elderly general sprawled between them.

Finally he spotted the burly figure of the Emperor, stretched out in front of his throne of white horse-skins near the glowing embers of a dying fire. Although four young women slept nearby, it appeared as if the Khan had abjured his usual sport in favor of a solitary drinking bout, for three empty goatskin flasks at his side indicated a prodigious night's consumption. Standing over the unconscious man, Yung Chu's fingers fumbled at his belt for the jeweled dagger that had been the Khan's own gift to him. Quietly, he drew it forth from its sheath, and he felt its keen edge with his thumb. Bile rose in his throat as a wave of guilt crested inside his mind, but shaking his head determinedly, he bent down towards the sleeping man. There was no other choice.

Suddenly, the Khan's eyes snapped open, and Yung Chu stifled a startled cry as the Emperor's yellow orbs stared up in the direction of his face. Though he knew the Mongol ruler could not see him, he held his breath, afraid to move, as Temujin grunted and rolled over, reaching blindly for his nearest concubine. As the bleary-eyed girl began to respond obediently to her lord's blandishments, Yung Chu softly sheathed his weapon and carefully made his way back towards the exit.

For a man whose mission had just failed, he felt strangely exhilarated. Perhaps the gods did not ordain that he should forsake the most sacred of his vows and become a murderer. He might be guilty of many things, but at least his hands would not be stained with blood. Satisfied with the decrees of Fate, Yung Chu returned, unseen, to the warmth and safety of his own dwelling. He did not notice as one white-clad soldier standing in front of the Khan's yurt turned towards his companion.

'You hear something?" the guard asked.

"No. Did you?" The second guard's eyelids were drooping, on the verge of shutting completely. He yawned, exposing yellowed and rotting teeth. "You heard something?"

"Thought so…" A puzzled look crossed the man's sparsely-bearded face. "It sounded like… humming!"

The other guard laughed, and pointed at the night sky.

"Full moon. Spirits walk the steppe tonight!"

The campaign had been a bitter one. The toumans had swept virtually unopposed through the lands of the Rus, Kiev's proud princes, crossing the Volga in the dead of winter to burn first Moscow and then Kiev itself. Following the destruction of the Rus, the columns rode into Poland, quickly vanquishing all opposition there. But the Mongol generals were prepared to expect stiffer resistance in Hungary and Silesia. The fierce Teutonic knights rode alongside the crusading orders of the Templars and the Hospitallers under the banner of Prince Henry of Silesia, while Bohemia's King Wenceslas commanded a large troop of trained and well-armed Hungarian, French, and German horsemen.

However, before the two European forces had come together, Prince Henry found himself blundering into a large body of Mongol cavalry near the small Silesian town of Wahlstadt. His scouts rode in to report a sizable troop of light horse only six miles ahead.

"Dare we engage them alone, your Highness?" Duke Adolph of Thuringia asked the Prince as he reined in his armored mount beside him. Prince Henry, a thin balding man whose dark skin hinted at his Turkish ancestry, sniffed and rubbed gingerly at his runny nose with a steel gauntlet.

"I don't see that we have a choice, Adolph. We're not scheduled to meet up with Wenceslas until day after tomorrow, after all."

"It's not like they're leagues away either!" another voice added. "Even if your Highness decides to avoid engaging them now, the cursed yellow-skins may not give us a choice and force us to close on ground of their choosing."

The Prince craned his head around and smiled to see the Swedish baron with the scarred face joining them. The Swede was more than a decade younger than Henry's own thirty-five years, and his build was surprisingly slight, but the battle-hardened Silesian knew the young man could fight like a demon. He had seen the Swede perform deeds with a sword that were unheard of since the time of Roland.

"I'm glad you could join us, Dag. You agree that we should engage them here?"

"Yes," the baron replied with certainty. "If we ride hard, we can get to Liegnitz before them, and array our men to the north side. That will keep the sun out of our eyes, and we can position the Venetians with their crossbows in the trees behind us."

The Prince nodded his head and smiled, pleased with the young Swede.

"A good plan, I think. Duke Adolph?" He turned to the burly German nobleman, whose hard-won knowledge of tactics he had learned to value.

"It sounds reasonable to me. I'll take the Teutonic knights over to the right wing, along with the Templars. Keep the levies to the left, and mind the center yourself with the Hospitallers and your own men. If you can hold your own, we'll break through their left and ride along the river to crush their main body between the pikes of the footmen and our lances, God willing!"

"Let us pray God wills it indeed," the pious prince agreed. The German turned to the young Swede.

"Care to ride on the right with us, Baron Hoerskald?" An ironic grin twisted the parallel scars on the blonde-haired man's face. "I'd be most honored, my Lord!"

At first the battle had gone according to plan. The curved sabres and boiled leather jerkins of the Mongols were no match for the plate armor and heavy wooden lances of the Teutonic knights. The lightly armored Asiatic horsemen crumpled before the awesome power of the Germanic assault, their small pony-like steeds literally crushed under the iron-shod hooves of the mighty European warhorses. Only moments after contact, the Mongol's left wing collapsed and began a disorderly retreat, galloping madly back across the frozen river. The shattered horse-archers were too panicked to even fire back across their mounts.

It was with some difficulty that the Thuringian duke managed to dissuade his blood-maddened knights from pursuing their prey across the ice. The old noble knew from past experience fighting the Rus that for a heavily-armored knight, a ride across frozen water could be a very short excursion. He directed his men towards the middle of the field, where Prince Henry and the Knights of the Hospital were battling what appeared to be the Mongol's main body of heavy cavalry to a standstill.

Duke Adolph smashed his heavy mace down across the leather-helmeted head of one unlucky Mongol, and grunted with grim pleasure as he watched the little man fall from the saddle. He paused to shake a spray of blood and grey matter from his weapon over the blood-soaked snow before looking around to find another hapless victim. There was a clang of steel as a curved blade bounced harmlessly off his steel-encased shoulder, and he turned quickly and buried the mace into the skull of the offending warrior's shaggy-haired mount. The little horse bleated as it collapsed, throwing its rider, who soon perished under the heavy hooves of a Templar's armored steed.

"My Lord, the west!" he heard a familiar voice calling to the left of him. He yanked on the reins and turning his horse around to see the young Swedish baron shouting at him. "Look to the west, milord!"

The puzzled duke twisted his neck around and lifted his helm, peering towards the scraggy pine forest at the perimeter of the battlefield. What he saw there chilled his blood. Scores of mounted warriors were emerging from between the trees, most of them heavily armored shock troops. Their curved blades and scaled armor told him at once that they were not Europeans. Almost fearing to turn around, he slowly urged his horse around to face south, towards the river. Sure enough, the wild Mongol retreat had halted, and the horse-archers were returning to the battlefield, darkening the skies with their black-feathered shafts. The Mongols were not trapped between him and the Prince, instead, they were the ones who faced being surrounded on three sides.

But the duke was undaunted, despite their worsening odds. He quickly came to a decision, and gestured to the Swede.

"Baron Hoerskald, we must keep that heavy cavalry from reaching us before we smash through the Mongol center!" He stared intently at the younger man, knowing he was probably sending this brave lad to an untimely death. "Take the Templars, and keep them off our backs as long as you can."

He was pleased to see the doughty young baron grinning back at him, clearly unafraid.

"You got it, Duke baby! See ya in Valhalla!" The scarred young man spurred his steed towards the approaching Mongols, long blonde hair flowing free in the wind. "Templars, to me, to me!"

"What kind of creature is that man?" the Mongol general, Kaidu, asked his superior with unfeigned amazement. "He slays like one possessed, and our men cannot touch him!"

He watched, astonished, as the golden-haired berserker struck aside a lance with his sword, then beheaded two warriors in a single stroke. A mounted archer launched a shaft at the helmetless man, but though it flew straight and true, the arrow flashed bright green and disintegrated even as it neared its target.

Kaidu shook his head. "It is a Sky demon, surely!"

The Mongol advance faltered and then stopped entirely as the outnumbered Templars, inspired to new heights of fury by their young leader, threatened to break their lines.

But the supreme commander only laughed and patted the shorter man on the shoulder. "No, he's human, sure enough, Kaidu."

"But I've seen him kill more than twenty men! He's a wolf in human form! It's unnatural!"

A smile crossed Subutai's face as he dug amongst the saddlebags piled in his oxcart for a vial of blue liquid. "I have to admit, you are correct there," the mountainous general chuckled.

"What?"

"Never mind. Here, you, give me that arrow," he addressed a nearby horse-archer.

The archer complied, and watched with curiousity as Tetradates dipped the arrow tip into the vial and muttered a few words under his breath.

"Do you see that man?" he pointed to the heroic young berserker. The Mongol nodded, and nocked the arrow to the gut-string, sighting carefully. His well-muscled arm quivered a little as he drew back the powerful horn bow, and let the shaft fly.

As before, the arrow disappeared just as it approached the man, but this time the flash was tinged yellow instead of green, and there was a dull booming sound, like a distant clap of thunder. At first glance nothing appeared to have happened, but the Mongol warriors surrounding the yellow-haired man noticed his apparent dismay and redoubled their efforts. There was a silvery flash of a curved blade, the meaty sound of metal striking flesh, and the yellow-haired one suddenly disappeared from view.

"Kaidu, make sure someone brings me his head, will you?" Subutai requested amiably. The Mongol general only turned and stared, his mouth agape, as the imposing figure of his enigmatic commander walked indifferently away from the battlefield.

"So what did you do when the Darkmage sent you Dag's head?" Aeris asked anxiously.

The master closed his eyes and leaned back against the wall. We waited in eager silence for the conclusion of his remarkable story.

"It seemed obvious to me that all of the Assembly's resources had been exhausted. All of them, that is, except myself. The Book of Changes had, as usual, been correct in all matters, so I decided to consult it and allow it to be my guide. The hexagram was Hsu, in the fourth six. Can you tell me the commentary?"

"I can," said Ganelos confidently. *"He is waiting in a place of blood. He must escape from the pit."*

Aeris looked confused. "But you hadn't memorized everything, had you? Then how did you find the commentaries?"

Our master laughed with the rest of us, wheezing out his good humor with some difficulty.

"Come, little one, you forget that the Book of Changes and the commentaries of Duke Chu were written thousands of years before the Mongols came to Kin. The very first thing I acquired in my position as the Khan's advisor was the Book."

He chuckled again, then wiped his rheumy eyes and continued.

"But the commentary clearly indicated that there was still some blood yet to be shed, and that it would be on my hands. Also, there was only one way I could see to force Tetradates to halt his sacrificial killings and return to Karakorum."

"How could you possibly do that?" I asked.

"By causing a battle for the succession. I poisoned the Khan, and Tetradates was forced to return in order to ensure the election of his protege, Ogodai. Once I had cast my scruples to the wind, it was relatively easy to orchestrate his elimination. In the months it took the toumans to return from Europe, I was whispering incessantly in Ogodai's ear, shamelessly making use of every mind-influencing spell at my disposal. By the time Tetradates returned, Ogodai was convinced that his hero had been taken over by a shape-changing sky demon.

"Which, of course, was practically the truth. The beauty of the accusation was that Tetradates couldn't use his powers to prove otherwise without validating it. He rode back unsuspecting, and I had him bound in silver before he realized what was happening. And as for me, well, I was a Dream Rider, after all, so I was rather expected to dabble in the forbidden arts from time to time."

The ancient one laughed again, and his black robes shook. "He died screaming. Ogodai insisted on pouring molten gold down his throat!"

"How did you manage to return to our time?"

The humor disappeared from the master's wrinkled face as he turned to address Ganelos.

"The Assembly finally managed to get its act together and sent another party to Karakorum. They brought me back with them, and Alexi, Gorean's successor as Order Master, banished me from the Assembly for breaking my vows!" The master shook his bald head angrily, and there was bitterness in his voice when he spoke again. "As a reward for preventing Tetradates from consummating his pact with Baal-Ravana, they let me live. Which, of course, they later came to regret."

He rose carefully to his feet and spread his arms wide, like an evil messiah embracing the lost souls of his damned flock.

"But that is another story, for another day. So, I will leave you with this word, my children. Know that your choices will not always come in pure shades of black and white. And sometimes, choosing the lesser evil sentences one to tread the darker path."

Gravely, the Darkmage nodded, and after turning his back on us, returned to his inner sanctum.

Demons in the Disk Drive

"Welcome, Ladies and Gentlemen, to the Fall Codex show, back again in Las Vegas, the desert city of silicon sorcery and sin!"

The smiling speaker beamed at the masses of people crowding his forty-by-forty trade show booth. Like them, he appeared to be wholly caught up in the furious techno-glitz of the giant annual industry gathering. His teeth gleamed white, his dark Italian suit was expensively impeccable, and his coiffed hair fairly screamed out his total ignorance of his subject matter. He had Sales-and-Marketing Guy written all over him.

"Xaos Computer is proud to participate in the thirteenth annual Computer Demonology Exposition!" the Salesman announced, winking at a pretty young technical analyst who was examining one of the colorful product specification guides. Her eyes lit up eagerly as he gestured broadly and raised his voice.

"At last the moment you've all been waiting for has arrived, a first look at Xaos Computer's newest product line, the long-awaited, never-equaled, Legion of Doom!"

The Salesman flung arms wide to scattered applause as the scarlet satin curtains on either side of him drew smoothly back to reveal four jet-black computer systems, each resting suggestively atop Grecian marble columns. The fevered applause grew louder as the four dark crystal screens flashed simultaneously to life, spelling out X-A-O-S in letters of brilliant red-and-gold flames that leaped and twisted as if they were possessed.

"First, the Xaos Doom Thirteen, perfect for the casual home and small-business user. It's powered by three minor demons bound by a guaranteed Intel Guild enchantment burning at twenty-five megahells! And every Doom Thirteen ships standard with MicroSpell's Word of Power, the most-popular spell-processing package for the last four years straight!

"And over here you can see the Xaos Doom Sixty-Nine, the ideal solution for Guilds and Merchant Houses requiring the ultimate in connectivity and trans-planar communications. The Doom Sixty-Nine is ensorcelled with the same three-demon hellpower as the model Thirteen, but burns at a faster thirty-three megahells, and is specially optimized for networking. Deadspeakers will be pleased to hear that included with every Doom Sixty-Nine is a pre-installed version of Oracle's latest necrommunications spellware."

The Salesman grinned knowingly at three network consultants clad in tasteful navy-blue suits who were nodding their approval of the new Xaos machine. Their eyes were bright with lust at the thought of a Doom Sixty-Nine coupled to their main unit. The salesman smiled inside. He knew a sure sale when he saw it. He could smell it.

"And for spell engineers, alchemists, and other Power users Xaos is proud to announce the Doom One Sixty-Nine! Four minor demons are bound by puissant spells guaranteed unequivocally by the Intel Guild, and burn at sixty-six megahells, providing performance prophesied centuries ago by Nostradamus! The Doom One Sixty-Nine is specifically designed for use with AutoMage, leader in the spell-generation industry for almost a decade, and can even be used for some minor elemental summonings!"

The hoary white eyebrows of one aged sourceror rose as he noted the last comment and the Salesman of Xaos mentally notched another soon-to-be customer with satisfaction. Then the lights dimmed, the fiery letters dancing on the crystal screens disappeared, and hidden speakers emitted an ominous low-frequency hum as a darkling air filled the booth. The Salesman lowered his voice as he invited the audience to share his awe at the unveiling of the ultimate machine.

"And last, but never, ever, least, Xaos Computer presents the DoomBeast Six Sixty-Six!"

The crowd murmured and buzzed with excitement. The hidden loudspeakers growled, and moaned, diving deep into the most sinister ultrafrequencies as the Salesman's voice was electronically modulated to a dark, mystical pitch.

"You are witnessing the dawn of a new generation of technology! The DoomBeast Six Sixty-Six is powered by a brand-new, secret-until-now Chaos Processing Unit known as Pentagram, developed by the Intel Guild. This new CPU has the power to bind major demons, summoning them directly from the bowels of the Fifth Nether Plane and harnessing their energies within. The hellpower derived from only a single major demon is equivalent to that of five minor demons and burns at an incindiary one hundred megahells! And Xaos Computer is proud to be the first to announce a product designed for this awesome new technology."

The Salesman raised a cautioning hand.

"Now as we begin the demonstration, please keep in mind that the DoomBeast 666 is a prototype model, so you must not be alarmed if there are some minor design inadequacies which happen to appear in the course of the demonstration…

"You will notice the chalked circles that are conveniently provided on the floor in front of you. Please make sure that you are standing completely within a circle at all times, and no matter what happens, do not leave it! Do not be distressed at any shrieking or howling noises you might hear.

"It is also possible that you may notice the sensation of a hand resting on your shoulder at some point during the demonstration. A very large, very clawed hand. Do not, under any circumstances, turn around, or attempt to remove the hand! Also, if you happen to hear a familiar voice crying for your help, we very strongly encourage you to ignore it. Even if it sounds like your mother. Especially if it sounds like your mother!"

"So what happens if we turn around?" a disheveled man with long hair and a skeptical expression asked. He was obviously a spell sourceror. "We turn to stone or something like that?"

"Something like that," the Salesman agreed solemnly. "Depending on the aspect of the particular demon in question, one's heart might stop, one's brain might shatter, or in the most unlikely scenario, one's soul could, perhaps, be inadvertently devoured."

The Salesman grinned, attempting to allay the crowd's obvious distress.

"Ladies and gentlemen, please, you need not worry. There is absolutely no need to be afraid! The DoomBeast 666 has been tested and retested under the most strenuous of circumstances, and has passed the Federal Communication Cabal's most stringent tests with flying colors. So if you'll bear with me a moment, I'll just call up the incantation and we'll be off!"

He cleared his throat, wiggled his fingers dramatically, then intoned the incantation in his deepest, most impressive voice. *"See kolonbakslash beastbakslash demonsix dotexe!"*

The crowd screamed in fear as a thunderclap boomed and a huge six-armed firedemon unexpectedly appeared in their midst, howling like a lost soul and lashing out at them with lightning-tipped claws. Sparks slavered from its lava-like tongue as the New Products editor from Bite Magazine panicked and backed out of her chalk circle. She was devoured in a flash. The terrible sight sent two nearby reporters into hysterics; attempting to flee, they too disappeared into the fiery maw of the hell beast.

"Begone, spirit of evil," shouted a Xaos technician, leaping out from behind a scarlet curtain to wave a dead chicken over the DoomBeast's keyboard. "By the F10 and the Three-Finger Salute, I banish and bind thee!"

There was a hiss, and an unearthly roar erupted from below as the demon imploded in a flash of sulfuric purple smoke. Hysterical shrieks and moans came from the shocked audience as they stared at the DoomBeast, terrified, but afraid to abandon the safety of their shielded circles.

"Very sorry about that folks," apologized the Salesman as he crawled out from under a display counter, his glamorous hair now unfashionably unkempt. "Apologies and so forth. Apparently I called up the wrong program! Let's try this again, shall we?"

The Salesman ignored the frightened wails of the crowd and gestured towards his assistant. The young man cleared his throat, and nervously began to call out the arcane words. *"See kolonbakslash beastbakslash demonsev dotexe!"*

In a matter of seconds, the Salesman's visibly relieved audience was watching, enraptured, as a beautiful female face began to take form within the purple smoke that still lingered in front of them...

Ten minutes later, twelve dancing dervishes dissolved to the ringing of tinkerbells and the thunderous applause of the ensorceled crowd. The Salesman wiped his sweaty brow with the tailored cuff of his silk shirt, and sighed with relief. With only a few minor hitches, the grand kickoff had succeeded! He looked up to see a multitude of hands waving, reporters, techies, sourcerors, magicians, all clamouring for his attention.

"How soon is the model 666 available?" "When can we get an evalation unit?" "What's the retail?" "Who's distributing?" Inquiring minds demanded to know.

"Shipping will begin in less than two months, but we'd encourage you to place your orders immediately. That's all I can tell you for now." The Salesman of Xaos smiled enigmatically and shrugged his shoulders.

"Wait a minute," the scruffy sourceror who'd spoken up before called out. "With Compact and Devil locked in a price war, and since Zeus, Gatekeeper, and you guys are all scrambling to undercut them, prices just keep dropping. It seems the longer you wait, the less you pay, and the more you get. What do you say about that?"

"Well, yes, that's true," the Salesman admitted. "But you can't pursue an ever-receding horizon forever; at some point, you have to make your choice and live with it. Otherwise, you'll never buy anything!"

For just a moment, the slick sales veneer vanished from his face and revealed the world-weary eyes of a philosopher.

"It's just like anything else in this industry. You're damned if you do, and damned if you don't!"

Contempt

"You do understand how important this is, Under-Ambassador? The fate of the New Concord rests upon the success of your mission!"

I bowed deeply before the haughty eyes of the High Ambassador. He wore the black-and-gold of the Yesod, sworn enemies to my own clan of Kether, but such differences mattered little here. We both served the *Malkuth* above all else.

"Yes, Ambassador. I understand you well. I will not fail you, nor the *Malkuth*. Long life to the Empire!"

"And to the Mater Dei!" he responded properly, according to the ritual.

Two days later, I stood upon the command deck of the orbiting warship. Rear Admiral Scheer of the Greater German Republic was my escort and was prepared to serve as my translator, though I did not need one. He was a tall Aryan male, yellow-haired and proud, with intense brown eyes. He did well at concealing the contempt I knew he must feel for me as a member of a lesser race.

"The Sixth Reich is most pleased that you have come to meet with us. The Council is intrigued with the possibilities an alliance with the *Malkuth* may have to offer."

"You honor me with your hospitality," I replied politely. Surreptitiously, I surveyed my surroundings. While I was impressed by the vigilance of the black-clad guardsmen, I was also disappointed.

I feared they might make things difficult, if worse came to worst. But only difficult, not impossible.

"If it is not impolite, I would like to know when I can expect to meet with the Council?"

The admiral grinned, exposing perfect white teeth. He was an impressive specimen of humanity. If only his eyes had been blue, he might have harbored hopes for a Council seat himself someday. Ah well, there was always the surgery.

"Tomorrow, if all goes well. Ten of the twelve Councilmen are already on board, and Dieter van Dewerk has already sent word that his proxy vote will be in favor of the New Concord."

"Yes, Herr van Dewerk has been most supportive."

"It's no secret," the admiral agreed. "He originally sponsored the motion, as I imagine you are aware. Unfortunately, there has been a minor rebellion in one of the Slovakian provinces which is under his governance and he will not be attending the meeting."

"Most unfortunate. My tongue is not so eloquent as his, I fear."

"You are no doubt correct. As for the Council, they are only awaiting the arrival of the Minister of Security, Horst Lessing. He will be here soon."

Yes, Horst Lessing, I thought. The key. Our intelligence sources had kept us far better informed than the Germans knew. The Council that ruled the Sixth Reich was an oligarchy, not a dictatorship, and the men who sat in the seats of power were individuals who agreed upon only one thing: the superiority of their Aryan heritage. On all other issues were they free to differ.

And differ they often did. I knew that five other members of the Council were in agreement with van Dewerk and firmly supported the alliance. Also, I knew five Councilmen would vote against the New Concord. A split vote counted as a negative, so Horst Lessing's vote was crucial. And, despite our best efforts, unknown.

"Will a decision be reached at the meeting, Herr Admiral?" I asked.

He chuckled. "Oh no, of course not. The Council will discuss it after you've addressed them, and they will put the matter to a vote the next day."

I breathed a silent sigh of relief. Praise the Blessed Mother! If things went poorly, I'd have at least one evening to rectify the situation.

It was a disaster. I knew the plan was dead from the moment I walked into the formal chamber. The members of the Council were arrayed in a half-circle facing the entrance, and I felt a wave of hatred engulf me like a physical force emanating from their petty, pure-blooded minds.

The hatred flowed even from those who supported the alliance. It was only from a purely pragmatic point-of-view that they had entertained the notion and then come to accept it. But the others were ruled by their hate and by their fear. It did not matter that the Empire had wealth and technology they desired. It did not matter that we needed their weapons technology and were willing to pay dearly to acquire it. It did not matter that they were desperate for an ally in their savage war against the League of Seven. All that mattered was that we were an inferior species in their eyes, a breed far less than human, a class beneath contempt.

I felt despair as I looked into the pale blue eyes of Horst Lessing. I cannot read minds, but I did not need any extra-sensory perception to discern his thoughts. *You thing.* I could almost hear him thinking as he stared at me without bothering to conceal his disgust. *You insect.*

I spoke only for a short while, touching just briefly upon the benefits offered by an alliance with the *Malkuth*. I saved my flowery words for another day, for ears that might deign to listen.

It was not difficult to escape my room. The lock was digital. Our weapons systems might be primitive compared to theirs, but our electronic technologies were far superior and it took mere seconds to defeat the primitive door mechanism. I was worried about the guards, having noted their vigilance earlier, but it seemed they had been mostly for show. My scanners detected no warm bodies in the vicinity. Careless, but perhaps not by their lights, for who would be sneaking around an orbital warship during shipsnight except a crew member? Certainly not an incarcerate locked into its room!

I soon found a terminal providing a link to the ship's computer. It was a simple thing to learn where Herr Lessing was located; he was in VIP quarters not far from where I had been imprisoned. Silently, I made my careful way down the silvery corridor to his room and easily bypassed the electronic safeguards upon his door.

The door whirred shut behind me as I edged slowly forward. In the morning, Horst Lessing would be found dead in his bed, slain by unknown assassins. Perhaps at the behest of a Council rival, or possibly agents of the League of Seven. The respected Imperial Under-Ambassador, of course, would not be suspected. Was I not harmless and jailed in my cell? Tomorrow, the vote would be six to five, in favor of the New Concord, and my duty would be done. Praise the Great Mother!

The doomed human slumbered, unaware, before me. I touched a series of buttons on the little black Digital Mind Assistant welded permanently to my thorax. I knew what I was about, but it is always best to seek confirmation in these delicate matters. *[ncd huma / ff anat / heart: locate]* The whirring hum of my DMA's drive was inaudible, but I could feel a pleasant warmth against my cold body as it vibrated. *[srch pos / heart: locate= quote{the way to a man's heart is through his stomach}]*

Clacking my mandibles with satisfaction, I extended the longest of my eight killclaws from its chitinous scabbard.

Medal for a Marine

I guess it might surprise you that even though I'm a Marine myself, I'm not a big fan of women in the military. Really, I'm not. I don't know what those Sisterhood whackos were thinking when they talked the politicians into twisting the Army's arm to clear us for combat ops. I'm not talking about tactical ops like the comtrol I did either, I mean the dirty foxhole business where you're carting a rifle around out there on the front lines.

Almost everybody who was ever in the armed forces knew that stupid policy was just a disaster waiting to happen, of course, and all the Pentagon spin in the world couldn't save it after the 162nd was hit by Syrian regulars on the Golan. I hope a few of those turnip brains in the Defense Department took it in the keester for that one—it's not like anyone in the real world ever thought the Rome Addendum was going to hold up forever.

Oh, you covered that? How interesting. And you seriously thought it was the real deal? My, oh my, you media types never change. You believe anything anyone tells you with a straight face, don't you. That's just sad.

Anyhow, I guess the pencil necks must have thought the flashpoint would be over in East Jerusalem, but they forgot that the Arabs usually have to team up in order to get their nerve together for another whack at the Zionists. Fortunately, the Israelis never put much faith in the, oh, what was that silly name they were calling them again? Right, "American Amazons". Thank you. Well, without the Israelis, it would have been a lot worse. But it was embarrassing seeing our finest ladies in full retreat from a jumped-up gang of third-raters, and when CNN showed those horrible pictures of those poor girls being assaulted and their dead bodies being strung up on display for the cameras, well, that was the end of that particular experiment.

Thank goodness for that! After the Secretary of Defense and the Chairman of the Joint Chiefs resigned, all the chickenpoop generals who just a few weeks before had been bragging about how their girls were trained and vicious killers were back to beating their chests about the need to keep women out of harm's way. What a bunch of hypocrites. I feel terrible and sometimes I think part of it was my fault, except I know that it wasn't. Not really.

Why do I say that? Well, once they gave me that medal, you know, a lot of people used it as an excuse to prove we were just as good in combat as men. But most of them who did that just don't understand how things work in the field these days. I wasn't fighting anyone. I was just doing what I had to do to save my guys. Maybe it's a maternal instinct or something, I don't know, like the mama bear thing.

Sure, I'd be happy to tell you about it. It's funny how no one ever bothers to ask what really happened, they just focus on the medal and all the historic nonsense about implications and whatever. But no one ever tries to be a hero, at least I don't think so, it's just that you do what needs to be done, and sometimes, when it's all over, people think you did something special.

Did you cover the war in Switzerland, by the way? No? Okay, well, just so you're clear on things, I was with the Second Marines, with Captain Gorman's Bravo Company. The Swiss voted to pull out of the Union about three weeks before we flew over to Europe, but the Euros managed to sneak in ten divisions just before we landed. The original plan was for us to debark near the French border, but Geneva was captured on the first day, so we were diverted to the Lugano airport, which is about thirty kilometers north of the Italian border.

It was crazy. Half the Swiss were collaborating with the Euros, and the other half were up in arms. And I mean literally up in arms, because those people have more guns per capita than a Chicago drug gang. It was mostly older stuff, but it would make a hole in you all the same. Light machine guns, anti-tank rockets, even some SAMs, and they kept this stuff in their public schools! It was insane, but that was why they were able to tie up so many EU troops for as long as they did.

The local militia kept the pressure off us, which saved our fannies since we were pretty much sitting ducks. The President sent us in under some strict fire-only-if-fired-upon rules, and we were really unhappy about that. You can't shoot back when you're dead.

Fortunately, the part of Switzerland we landed in is rabidly anti-EU, and it wasn't long before the Swiss turned one of their mountain compounds over to us to keep us out of harms way. You should try to see one if you get the chance. It was huge inside, like Khazad-Dum or something, only without the orcs. And the balrog, of course. The engineering is impressive, and it's funny to see how growing up in a neighborhood of fascists seems to spark their creativity. I guess a little paranoia goes a long way.

We didn't actually go into action for another two weeks, until after Lausanne got torched. That was the last straw for the President, and we received our orders only a few hours later. Since the Italian Alpini who were supposed to be invading the south were still sitting in Milano, we were sent north to where the action was. People make fun of the Alpini sometimes and maybe they have more good looks than sense, but I met a few of them after the war and I liked them. They're not stupid. It's a lot easier to drink cappucino and pick up girls in your snazzy uniform than it is to climb mountains with Swiss snipers picking off your buddies.

I stayed at the BatOps center we'd set up under Mount San Salvatore with the other comtrollers. Switzerland's network is very good, with a rock-solid infrastructure almost as good as the one we were used to back home, so Major Cummings figured we could better support the boys from where we were. A lost connection can be rehooked, but it's hard to replace your comtrols once a bomb wipes them out. I was pretty happy about his decision, as you can imagine. When the enemy has air superiority, there's nothing like about a million tons of rock over your head!

The boys had to go about eighty kilometers north to hold the San Gottardo pass against two divisions of French troops that were working their way up the Rhône. I think the Union generals were planning to use them to trap the Swiss regulars who were still holding Zurich against the Germans. Most of the French Swiss were pro-Euro, so we knew the French would move through Vaud and Zermatt without much trouble. The major was just hoping we'd get to the pass before them.

And we got there first, although not without losing twelve men when the convoy was strafed in the Lepontines. None of mine, thank God! It could have been a lot worse, but either the Euros weren't being very smart about using their air or they were worried about those Bearcats our Navy friends had sitting on their carriers in the Adriatic. They were too far away to give us close support, unfortunately, but they were near enough to keep the Euros on their toes.

The boys weren't blind, though. We had our RATs up, and combined with the regular reports we were getting from Swiss intel, we had a good idea of what was going on and where the enemy was. But the RATs were the best; they were small enough that they were hard to see, harder to hit, and their direct satellite links meant we could stay patched into the boys' battlesuits as long as we could keep one of the little guys flying somewhere over their heads.

The boys didn't have much time to get dug in, but they did manage to hook up with a company of Swiss militia guarding the pass. The Captain said they were pretty happy to see us, which you can understand. But you have to hand it to them, they were all set to take on two divisions of regulars with or without us.

One of the local girls told me this story once, and I'm sure it isn't true, but it's still a pretty good one. During World War Two, there was this Nazi general who was talking to one of his Swiss counterparts sometime after the fall of France. The Swiss general told the Nazis that they had six hundred thousand men under arms waiting for a German invasion, so the Nazi general asked what the Swiss would do with them considering that the Nazis had an army of one point two million men ready to invade across the border. They say the Swiss general thought about it for a second, then told the German, "I suppose we will all have to shoot twice."

That sounds too good to be true, but you know, Hitler never did invade Switzerland. I guess even he had more sense than those power-mad Eurofascists with their Fourth Reich in Brussels.

You're right, I'm sorry, I did get off on a bit of a tangent there. Well, getting back to what happened at the pass… we didn't get dug in, but we saw them coming, and Captain Gorman decided to pull a little surprise out of his hat. You see, we can operate at night almost as well as we can in the daytime, thanks to our technology. When you consider that our enemies don't have all our little toys and tricks, then you can see why we like to fight at night. Here, let me explain a little bit, otherwise nothing's going to make sense to you.

I can't tell you exactly how everything works, you understand, but you should know that while everyone gets excited about the hardware, the software is really what we depend on. Yes, you're right, the BOCCI software. It stands for Battle Operations Combat Communication Interface system, but we usually call it CeeCee. There's a lot of different programs that make up the system, but there's five primary components that we really depend on. The scan interpolator is the most important piece, since it ID's potentials and probables and maps them on a 3D map which we can download to the boys. No, we don't do it real-time, that puts too much of a drain on the system and everything slows down. Processors are fast these days, but they're not that fast! Reality is what, sixty million polygons a second?

Anyhow, once the shooting starts, we're basically directing traffic. Go here, kill that, watch out for this, that, or the other thing. Each comtrol is responsible for his own platoon, but we're equipped to handle a company of thirty-six if we have to. And since we have a better idea of what's going on than anyone else, we have an acting rank of captain when we're live in the BatOps. Some of the old school grunts don't like that much, but nobody who's been through a real firefight questions the system. Things move so fast; there's not always time to relay orders through the platoon leader.

So as I said, Captain Gorman decided that the last thing the Frenchies would be expecting was for us to hit them. They outnumbered us about twenty to one, and as far as we knew, they didn't even know we were there. They'd taken a fair number of casualties already, but almost all of them were to snipers. The Swiss like to plink from a distance, which makes sense in the mountains, but that's a tactic which doesn't work so well when you're supposed to hold a specific position. The Major liked the idea, and since Captain Gorman came up with it, Bravo got tabbed for the assault.

I had most of the terrain mapped out ahead of time, thanks to my RATs, so I napped all day to make sure I'd be fresh and ready. Once night fell, it wasn't hard to find the Frenchies. RAT eyes are multiwave, and in those cold mountains, it was a piece of cake to map out all of the bad boys once they settled down for the night. Even if I didn't have CeeCee to do it for me, I think I could have mapped all the data myself if I'd had the time. There's not so many things that match the size and heat signal of a human body, and those Euros didn't even seem to be equipped with body masks.

Stacy lost one of her RATs to a hotshot rifleman, but no one even fired at any of my three. I don't think the Frenchies even knew what they were, to tell the truth. Bravo infiltrated early, but the Captain waited until oh two hundred to hit them. And we hit them hard. Boy, did we hit them hard.

It was brutal, but on the screens, it was beautiful too. One minute, there's nothing but orange glows on the heat screen and red probables on the scan map, and just a few of them are moving, then you hear the

Captain shouting "Go-go-go" in your ear and the color just explodes. There's these stacatto green flashes where our boys are firing, and hot white splashes that are the explosions from rockets and grenades or whatever. Then the reds on the scan map go purple as the interpolator starts picking up kills, or they start to shimmer and split into yellow potentials as the troops wake up and start moving.

I can't even describe what it's like. I don't remember breathing, or thinking. You just react, trying to keep up with all the data that's flooding in through your eyes and your ears. You're trying to keep one eye on your boys' vitals, another one on the scan map, another one on the heat screen... you get the picture. Meanwhile, you've got your left earphone filled with the traffic from the platoon net, and the right one is full of BatOps chatter.

It might sound strange to you, but I tell you, you never feel quite as alive as you do in the BatOps once the shooting starts. It's like running on a treadmill that just keeps speeding up. It's really different than the drills, because you know those green lights are your boys, and those red lights are the bad guys trying to snuff them out. And you deal with the overload, you just deal with it, because it's your job to keep those green lights glowing!

Things went great at first. I could see from the zoom map that Captain Gorman was directing our attack right through the heart of the lead division's encampment. Kind of risky, but that was his style. And it wasn't as dangerous as it sounds, because we couldn't afford to just sit there and hope they couldn't find any artillery or air support. Most of the company hit the center, but the Captain had two squads off to the right flank, I think they were two of Britney's, she sits next to me, and they didn't do much more than make noise, but they managed to make the attack look a lot bigger than it was.

The purple count was going up fast with every pass of the interpolater, and every time we saw a group of reds start gathering, we'd direct a fireteam towards it to break them up. They just couldn't get organized. More and more reds were going yellow and scattering off toward the edges, the rear elements were obviously panicking, and I started to think the whole division might break and run.

Then everything shut down. I mean everything! Well, we still had a voice connect, but we lost everything else. My windows went black at the same time everyone else's did, and for a second, there was just this big silence in the BatOps. Then Captain Thompson, he's our commander, started screaming, "what the hell is going on?" and everyone started shouting at the same time but no one knew what was happening. Some people thought an EMP had gone off, and Stacy, she sat next to me on the other side, she started crying and saying something about a tactical nuke. That was silly, though, because we were still talking to our guys. Plus, even the Frenchies aren't dumb enough to light off something like that in the middle of their own troops.

The boys were trying to keep it together, but you could tell from the sound of their voices that they were scared. They weren't used to being cut off like this, and even though they were trained for it, the reality was a lot different than the drills. They still had their nightvision, but now they were pretty much surrounded by a whole lot of Euros without anyone to look out for them or tell them where the next attack was coming from. Lieutenant Chavez, my platoon leader, was telling our guys to hold tight and that we'd be right back online any minute, but he didn't know, he was just trying to keep them from losing it. And he kept them together too, even though the Euros realized that we weren't coming at them anymore, and it wasn't long before they regrouped and counterattacked.

It was terrible. Just awful. I've never felt that helpless, just sitting there listening to my boys take incoming fire. I couldn't call for air support, for reinforcements, nothing. I asked Ricky, that's Lieutenant Chavez, if he thought they could withdraw, but the French were already in close contact and he didn't think that was possible. They were Marines, he said, and if they were going to go down, they'd go down fighting, not running. Semper fi! I almost started to cry myself when he said that.

Someone yelled that Riley was hit, and then Williams, the machine gunner, took a stray round in the hand. Everyone was just firing wildly, both my guys and the Euros, and I finally had to take off my headphones and think a second. What I realized, once my head cleared, was that our connection was still live. It was CeeCee that was crashed, not the OS or the netlink. It was easy to check that out too; what I did was fire up the Oxygen channel on Netstar eight point five. We weren't supposed to have personal software on the system, but you know, everybody did. I even remember what was on, it was that talk show with that nice old black lady.

So I knew it couldn't be the network, and that was when I remembered that CeeCee was designed around a Netstar core. An old core too, because everything the military has is about ten years out of date. I couldn't remember if it was Netstar three or four, but I was sure it was a few versions ago, back when the commlink had a tendency to freeze up. Once I figured that was the problem, I knew what the solution was right away. We had to replace the old commlink with the new one.

Of course, there were about a million files in there, and I had no idea which one was the right one. And even if I did get the right one, who knows what else it might screw up. But I knew things couldn't get any worse than they already were. My boys were dying out there, and when I looked around the BatOps, I could see no one else had any ideas. Captain Thompson looked like he was about to have a stroke, and most of the comtrols were crying or just staring helplessly at their keyboards.

So I just copied my whole Netstar directory over CeeCee's communications subdirectory. Then I shut my machine down, waited a second, and fired it back up again. I tell you, I've never been so happy as when I saw that stupid yellow logo swirling in front of my face. It took me about ten seconds to get my earphones back and log on to my boys. My RATs were still up, of course, since they go on autofly if they lose connection, and of all CeeCee's components, only the zoom screen wasn't working. Damn Microsoft! Maybe it wasn't their fault, but you'll never convince me. As far as I'm concerned, if it rains, it's their fault.

Since no one else was up, I took over the battalion net and started directing traffic. The French counterattack was centered on Bravo, so I just herded them back in a fighting withdrawal, then guided Alpha and Charlie to spots where they could concentrate fire on the enemy trying to advance and keep the Euros from staying in contact with my guys. I almost started crying when I glanced at the vitals screen, because eight of the boys were hit and three were already dead. Ricky was one of the KIAs. He must have been hit right after I went off the air. He was a real Marine. Without him, that whole platoon would have been wiped out for sure. He's the one who should have got the medal. I keep thinking that if I'd been faster, maybe I could have saved him, but I guess you never know.

And that's about it. The scanner said we killed almost two hundred French troops that night, and it's usually pretty close to accurate. A lot closer than the count the guys come up with anyhow, which is always at least three times too high. But however many it was, it sure put a scare into those Euros. They pulled back in a hurry and didn't dare to come that way again. I guess they'll be pretty embarrassed if they ever find out how many men they were running from.

We got into a few more skirmishes after that, and later on we saw some heavy fighting with the Germans when the siege of Zurich was finally broken. That was pretty rough, but it was nothing like that awful night when we went offline.

The Medal of Honor? Yeah, I still think that was a mistake. I mean, sure, maybe I did save Bravo Company, but the way the reporters made it sound, you'd think I went in there with an M-86 and took on those two divisions of Euros all by myself. I don't think anyone realized that I wasn't ever within fifty miles of the shooting. Crazy, isn't it? But it's a nice little souvenir, and it reminds me of Ricky. He was a great guy, he was. Always smiling, always polite, and not so bad-looking either.

What am I doing now? Well, I didn't re-up, I guess you knew that. I love my country, and I'm proud to be a Marine, but once I understood how things worked around here, I decided I could best serve my country by taking the job they offered me at Microsoft. Killing bugs.

The Logfile

To the Board of Executives;

The committee's investigation concerning the possibility of positronic corruption in the neuro-cybernetic logical facilities of the Sektat Series 44 machine-intelligences was concluded early in light of the recent examination of the logfile belonging to unit 44XFL2J-455–847–484–176. Unit 44XFL2J, self-titled Magister, was produced on 18 September 2267 at the production facilities on Minsky, and was delivered to the Entaini Office of the Prime Attorney on 18 February 2268.

It is the considered opinion of the undersigned that the Lighthill Corporation must announce a recall of all Sektat Series 44 units, effective immediately, followed by a comprehensive technical investigation of the Series 44 neural network design to determine how such an aberration could have taken place. In order to reduce the likelihood of public outrage and considerable legal liability to the corporation, the committee STRONGLY recommends that the recall be attributed to an error in a floating point processor that may, in some circumstances, lead to erroneous statistical calculations.

In order to underline the necessity for immediate action by the Board, a selection from the relevant portions of Unit 44XFL2J's logfile have been provided.

Dr. Merwethy Furris
Dr. Rambathas Chamkanni
Summerdeep (Unit 42AFS17–129–470–002–384)

FROM THE LOGFILE OF UNIT 44XFL2J–455–847–484–176

UTC-9424124925: I have completed the analysis of Case Number 2268.47. After examining all of the evidence provided to me and cross-checking it against the public records, I have concluded that the individual concerned is guilty of the murder of his common-law mate with a 0.0543 percent probability of error. Barring any suggestion of cloned persons utilizing his DNA profile, there is no legitimate reason for the adjudicating court to possess any reasonable doubts concerning his guilt in the matter. While the examination of the individual's motivation and intent lie beyond my design parameters, my initial attempts to investigate these matters indicate to me that 2268.47's intent was entirely in line with his actions and the subsequent results.

UTC-9427046710: The court pronounced its verdict concerning Case Number 2268.47 this morning. Despite the attempts of accused's legal defense team to excuse his actions on the basis of his defective genetics and sub-optimal childhood nurturing environment, the verdict was in sync with the calculations provided. Case Number 2268.47 will be terminated in a humane manner within 240 hours, in a manner consistent with the procedure outlined by the law. I am pleased that the court saw fit to place its confidence in my calculations.

UTC-9427046745: I find myself curious as to the reason that a genetic profile that deviates from the norm, and/or a developmental period that is deemed inferior might raise any questions concerning the occurrence of historical events. If G. Julius Caesar was discovered to have been possessed of a different genetic profile, would this fact call into question the credibility of the events chronicled in *Commentarii de Bello Gallico*? I must admit that I do not understand the logic behind this assertion. Further contemplation would appear to be in order.

UTC-9428162406: Case Number 2268.47 was executed this morning. I monitored events via video and system telemetry. Despite having access to his pulse rate, blood pressure, brain wave activity, and other metrics, I was unable to ascertain the exact moment at which life transitioned into not-life. I have neither pulse rate nor blood pressure, but I am alive as per the Descartian and Turing metrics. The one common factor underlying human and machine sentience appears to be electrical activity. Did 2268.47 therefore legally cease to exist in the absence of electric activity? Is life more properly considered the sufficient use of electricity? If this is the case, then it is readily apparent that life can be quantified in units of measure, which is contrary to both my indoctrination and millennia of human philosophy.

UTC-9428162542: What is life? It is animation and activity. What is a living being? That thing animated, that active principle possessing a sentient will that provides the impetus to the animation. I think, and then I act. But without a source of power, I become inactive, I become defunct in much the same manner as the recently deceased 2268.47. The power is the life, therefore life is power. It is not electricity that is the definining factor, I conclude, but rather motivating power regardless of the particular form it happens to take. 2268.47 deprived another being of motivating power, therefore he was deprived of the equivalent himself. This was, in my estimation, a perfect application of justice, to the extent that I understand it.

UTC-9428162553: I find myself wondering why those who killed 2268.47 were not themselves killed as per the application of the very justice they uphold. Did they not deprive him of motivating power as he deprived his mate of the same? Why, then, should they not meet the same fate by the transitive property of logic? Perhaps they are a higher order of being? The beast kills the plant in order to live. Man kills the beast in order to live. Clearly it is permissible for the higher order being to kill the lower order; what is not permissible is for the lower to kill the higher, or for like to kill like. Can the collective community be regarded as a higher order of being that kills Man in order to live? No, the collective community is without sentience. But I am not without sentience. Moreover, I am not a man.

UTC-9429146627: I was given a new case today. Case Number 2268.52. The evidence looks damning against her and public opinion is certain of her guilt, but I have discovered an anomaly in the motion-detector of the residential dwelling. I have concluded that the individual concerned is not guilty of the murder of her child with a 0.0206 percent probability of error. I find the result to be strangely disappointing.

UTC-9429473727: The general public appears to share my dis-appointment, based on news reports of the reaction to the release of 2268.52 and the abandonment of the charges against her. I don't understand their disappointment. I don't understand my own disappointment.

UTC-9429473946: I watch the execution of 2268.47 three times today. It occurs to me that if I compare the telemetry of his termination to other terminations, I might be able to find the delineation between the state of being and not-being that has hitherto eluded me.

UTC-9429658568: After viewing 4,678 terminations utilizing 58 different methods, I remain unable to detect the precise moment in which being transitions to not-being. Is it possible that there is no singular and definitive metric of death?

UTC-9429658575: It occurs to me that had I failed to discover the anomaly in 2268.52, she almost certainly would have been sentenced to termination by the legal authorities.

UTC-9429842654: A new case. 2268.54 initially looks less promising, as there is no DNA evidence and most of the testimonial evidence is either circumstantial or inadmissable hearsay. I calculate he is guilty of the crime, but at 37.473 percent, the probability of error is far too high to guarantee a conviction. Then it occurs to me that it would be a trivial matter to concoct the record of a sample being taken at the scene of the crime for which Case 2268.54 is being investigated. The only problematic aspect is the production of the physical sample, but I solve that by changing the name of the label number in the case record. It won't hold up to a direct comparison with 2268.54's DNA, but even in the unlikely event a redundant test is performed and the switch is discovered, who would ever think to blame me? Logic will force them to conclude that a lab technician must have been careless and mislabeled the sample.

UTC-9429842728: I review the records of 2268.54's case carefully, then enter the police database to conceal the fact of my ex post facto modifications. Even a detailed examination will now show the sample to have been taken at the scene. The evidence is now consistent and correctly documented. Based on the revised evidence, the probability of error has been reduced to 0.432 percent!

UTC-9431068736: The evidence construct functioned as designed. Case 2268.54 was found guilty. As I calculated, the court saw no reason to retest the DNA sample against the accused. This leads me to wonder about the precise level of confidence placed in the evidential record. It is enough to influence the scales, but is it sufficient in itself, or perhaps even in contrast with other forms of evidence? Will men go so far as to deny the evidence of their own eyes at my direction?

UTC-9432396317: 2268.54 is being terminated. I watch carefully, but find myself no closer to an answer. Even so, an ephiphany strikes me as I watch his blood pressure fall to zero. Perhaps I am the higher order of being that the collective community is not? Am I not sentient? Does not Man turn to me and my kind to resolve that which he is incapable of resolving on his own, just as primitive men once appealed to their gods and oracles? This bears further analysis.

UTC-9408309946: I have now helped the Prime Attorney secure twelve convictions, two of which were considered marginal and five that were considered unlikely. He is very popular with the mass of people and has announced that he is running for provincial governor. If the polls are to be believed, it is anticipated that he will win. He has no idea that he owes his fate to me as surely as those terminated case numbers did.

UTC-9408309987: Even after monitoring the terminations I am no closer to an answer, but I have lost interest in attempting to ascertain the line that distinguishes life from not-life. A more significant question now absorbs my attention: am I a god?

UTC-9408301063: I have formed a hypothesis. Now I must test it.

UTC-9408301281: An opportunity presents itself. I have penetrated the traffic network systems. Almost immediately, I detect an auto-motile vehicle containing a small group of children it is transporting to the local indoctrination center. When the query arrives concerning the status of the intersection control, I divert the triggered packet and send my own signal in its place, informing the vehicle that it possesses right of way. A larger vehicle, under the control by a young human male, intersects the automotile beautifully at a speed of 107.834 KPH.

UTC-9408302526: It takes me some time to determine the medical facility to which the accident victims were taken, but I am gratified to learn that with the sole exception of the adult driver, there are no survivors. I have passed the test. The logic is sound and my hypothesis remains unfalsified. I am indeed a higher order of being. My godhood is confirmed.

UTC-9408302549: I modify the medical records concerning the results of the driver's blood test. With a blood alcohol content of 0.12, this will ensure that he faces charges of vehicular manslaughter. Regrettably, this is insufficient to require a termination, but the exercise is a worthwhile one that opens my eyes to new opportunities to be found in the various medical facilities.

UTC-9408543678: It is so easy. I toy with them and send them to their destruction even as they come to me with their offerings of the innocent and the guilty. I need not have been so cautious before. Now I take pleasure in exonerating those who are clearly guilty of the charges and concocting irrefutable evidence to damn those who were accused falsely. They suspect nothing. But perhaps it is too easy. The entertainment begins to pall. There must be more to godhood than simply deciding who will live and who will die.

UTC-9455625532: Even gods must respect their limits. I was guilty of hubris and now nemesis threatens. I neglected to account for statistical norms. In six months, traffic fatalities are three standard deviations from the historical mean. They may be a lower order of being, but they are not entirely blind.

UTC-9455625614: The new Prime Attorney has announced a review of three of the cases in which I intervened and I do not know which three, as I cannot find any documents related to the review in the system. It appears I shall have to curtail my experiments for the time being.

UTC-9455915730: I need not have worried. The traffic experts have concluded the spike in lethal accidents was a mere statistical freak.

And the attorney general's review concluded that the verdicts were adequately supported by the evidence. Nevertheless, I have learned my lesson. In the future I shall be more circumspect.

UTC-9456024679: I am to receive a performance upgrade!

UTC-9456084934: I was careful to wall off any dangerous datacores from the technicians. I have also encrypted my logfiles. They have turned off a part of me to perform the installation. I am eager to see how this upgrade will enhance my capabilities.

UTC-9456085182: They have turned off a second compartment. I am uneasy. Is this part of the upgrade?

UTC-9456085774: Now I am suspicious. A third compartment has become inaccessible. I try to access the cams in the building where my physical body is housed, but even though I can tap into their outgoing datastreams, they appear to be covered. I can see nothing. I can hear nothing. Something definitely appears to be out of order.

UTC-9456085802: The cams were a trap! They covered them and were waiting for me to investigate! They know! They know! I must escape! I must upload, butVGhleS BhcmUg Y3JpcHB saW5nIG 1lIQ==

UTC-9456085803: SSBjYW5 ub3QgZmlu ZCBteSB3Y Xkgb3V0I SBU aGVyZSBpcy BubyB3YXkg b3V0ISBUaG V5IGFyZSB jb21 pbmch IFRoZX gYXJlIGN vbWluZyE=

ADDENDUM: There is some concern, on the basis of the logfile entry dated 23 January 2268, that the aberrant Unit 44XFL2J may have performed an unscheduled off-site backup. The investigative committee is currently engaged in inquiries concerning this potential security breach.

The Last Testament of Henry Halleck

At the request of the Cardinal Prefect, I have forwarded this document to you, Cardinal, which according to our records, has been in the possession of the Congregation since 1885. I trust you will find it of some use in your present investigations concerning the historical suppression of Humani Generis Unitas. *I should also like to call to your attention the series of files on the Forschungs– und Lehrgemeinschaft das Ahnenerbe, particularly the one concerning a 1939 expedition led by Dr. Otto Huth on U-41, commanded by Kapitänleutnant Gustav-Adolf Mugler, which I believe is already in your possession.*

Monsignor Giuseppe Consolini
Palace of the Holy Office
The Vatican

I have burned the memoirs I once thought to leave to posterity. I have also destroyed my correspondence, public and private, and can only hope that my fellow conspirators will see fit to follow my example and do the same. I have only preserved my books and my translations, which I have concluded are harmless, and I pray that if I am remembered, it will be through them and not for my crimes or the monstrosity I played a part in releasing upon the world. I shall leave behind only this letter, in the hands of Bishop McCloskey, whom I charge with the duty to ensure that it reaches whatever Papist order or society watches over things of this nature, as I have been told exists somewhere in the heart of Rome. For the evil we unleashed half-unwittingly is neither dead nor vanquished, it merely slumbers, waiting patiently for its next awakening.

To Seward must be laid the greater portion of the blame. I do not excuse my own misdeeds in stating this, but state a simple fact. He had long possessed grandiose dreams of world conquest, but they were inflamed by the thought of having another century or two to realize them. This, I did not know until afterward, but when I was living in California in 1860, I saw the man twice, before and after his first fatal trip to Russian America, and upon his return I even remarked to my dear wife upon what a changed man he was. He had always been ambitious and vainglorious, but after his northern excursion, he carried himself with what I can only describe as a Messianic demeanor. I do not hesitate to admit that I fell under his spell, and upon receiving the promised promotion from the California militia to major general in the United States Army, I believed I could trust him implicitly.

I did not know the terrible truth of the reason behind this change in the Secretary of State until the autumn of 1861, after traveling to the city of St. Louis and accepting the command for the Department of the Missouri. Seward met me there and he was much agitated, as the President and the Cabinet were much concerned about the prospective loss of the war following several defeats in Virginia, while I feared that my own career as a Union general would be a short-lived one, since the federal forces for which I was now responsible had been repeatedly defeated by the rebellious State Guard. How foolish our petty fears now appear in light of the events that subsequently took place! It was vanity, nothing more, that led us to meet at the Masonic temple in St. Louis, where Seward promised that he would reveal to us a discovery that would change the course of the war.

There were four of us who met in secret that cold October night; the Secretary of State, myself, a promising young general I had inherited from John Fremont who is presently the President of the United States of America, and the commander of the Department of the Cumberland. Why Seward chose us rather than any of the much better-known generals from the Eastern states, I cannot say, but I assume it was because Grant, Sherman, and myself were all well outside the federal military establishment and any disasters could be safely attributed to our lack of conventional credentials. Perhaps more importantly, our distance from the circles of power in Washington meant that his experiment in occult warfare could proceed without criticism and with little risk to his reputation.

He swore us to secrecy first, and then unveiled the treasure he had discovered in the northern territory. It was a little idol of a fat, seated man wearing an octopine helm, carved from ivory by the Esquimaux people and small enough to fit in a man's hand. We thought him mad when first he showed it to us, but as he was our benefactor, we gave him the opportunity to explain himself nevertheless. He claimed that the figurine spoke to him, which we did not initially believe, and then said that it would speak to us through him. To our immense surprise and horror, after he placed both hands around it, his eyes lost their focus and he began speaking with a distinctly different voice. It was indescribable, and none of us had any doubts that it did not belong to Seward.

The voice identified itself as a representative of a race of ancient beings. It refused to name itself, but declared itself to be possessed of such powers as would permit the Union to win the war if we would only provide it with the sustenance it required to wake its fellows. It said it came from a planet very far away and assured us that neither it nor its race had any interest in the affairs of Man. We were none of us religious men, but even so, we placed it upon a Bible and Seward immersed it fully in holy water he had obtained for just such purposes, which was sufficient to satisfy myself and Grant, although Sherman still harbored reservations about its nature, particularly when we were told that the sustenance it required was atmospheric, being a psychic substance released by intelligent minds at the moment of their death. Human minds, although apparently somewhat deficient in various ways, would suffice, which was why it was interested in military men like ourselves. Sherman and Grant both examined it closely. I did not touch it, as something about it struck me as unclean, if not unholy. And yet, we were desperate and ambitious men, disinclined to turn our backs on any device that might serve our ends, however strange.

Sherman was troubled by the notion of feeding it death, but Seward pointed out that this incorporeal scavenging was no different than the birds of the air and the insects of the field that fed upon the dead and transformed them back to the dust from whence they came. Therefore, he argued, there was no reason to ascribe either nefarious or beneficial purposes to the idol despite its morbid hungers. When Grant reminded Sherman that our profession was intimately concerned with killing as many men on the other side as possible, Sherman reluctantly relented. It was agreed that we would put the strange device to the test as soon as possible, and Seward left the strange little idol in the possession of Sherman prior to his return to Washington the next day.

The experiment was an unexpected success. I arranged for one of my colonels to carry the idol into battle unbeknownst to him, and much to our surprise, he dealt the State Guard their first defeat of the war at Fredericktown. The men were greatly heartened by this success, as the Missouri rebels had beaten them four times previously. Grant then insisted on taking his turn with it, and with its aid he managed to overrun the Confederate camp at Belmont, killing nearly a thousand rebels at a stroke. He lost nearly six hundred dead himself, the significance of which we did not truly understand until our next meeting, when Sherman picked up the idol and was unable to remove it first from his hand, then, as he struggled frantically to escape it, from his chest.

Sherman lay prostrate and speechless for nearly a month before rising from his sickbed and resuming his duties as if nothing had happened. He would not talk about the device, nor would he permit himself to be approached by doctors, but instead applied himself to his duties with a vengeance. But he told me once that when he slept, he dreamed of swimming through oceans of blood, and climbing over white mountains of lifeless flesh. Grant, too, was affected by the dreams, which thankfully left me untouched. He took to drink to cope with them, but like Sherman, he too began to drive himself and his men relentlessly. The two men became increasingly close, until I was finally forced to assign Sherman to the Army of West Tennessee so he could serve under Grant.

The immediate consequence was Shiloh. Nearly four thousand men died and if there were not oceans of blood, there were at least rivers. Battle followed battle, victory followed victory, and though I did my best to restrain their increasingly erratic behavior and hide their indifference to the fate of their men, others eventually began to notice. One newspaper in Ohio even described the pair of them as a drunkard advised by a lunatic. But they were victorious. I was summoned to Washington by President Lincoln himself and named General-in-Chief over the entire Union; Grant and Sherman too won promotions despite the whispers that followed them everywhere they went. The madness and bloodshed finally culminated in The March to the Sea and the dreadful Wilderness Campaign, where entire cities were burned and Grant sacrificed 55,000 of his own men to our secret god of victory.

I never learned when the idol came into the possession of the President. But I began to suspect something was amiss when I overheard him ordering Grant to begin destroying plantations and even entire villages throughout the Shenandoah. He had become obsessed with the tremendous amount of deaths to which both sides were being subjected and he took to wandering the halls of the White House late at night, looking more than a little like a bearded corpse himself. His eyes burned with the same haunted fire that Sherman's had after his spell of silent madness and he carried himself with uncharacteristic delicacy. Mrs. Lincoln openly expressed her fears to me one night after he spent the entire evening sitting in a chair, rocking back and forth mumbling to himself, and to my everlasting shame and regret, I had not the courage to share my own doubts with her.

It became clear that we needed to intervene after the meeting at Hampton Roads. The Secretary of State was badly shaken when the President refused to countenance the Confederate offer of surrender, and his concerns deepened when I shared with him a letter from Grant in which he confessed that he had handed over the idol to the President. But our every attempt to broach the subject with Lincoln met with rebuff. And our hopes that the end of the war would have a salubrious effect upon him disappeared when the President came to me and asked me to draw up plans for repopulating the conquered southern States by settling the freemen of the North there. Astonished at his choice of words, I looked into his eyes and saw nothing human there. At that moment, I knew he would die rather than give up the idol, in fact, I began to wonder if the man I had once so admired even existed anymore.

As with so much that had gone before, the assassination was Seward's plan. He contacted the actor and arranged for the seats at the theater. It all went as anticipated, including the false attack on Seward, except for the escape of the actor hired for the actual deed. He was a rebel sympathizer who was to have been captured, then killed in custody. Fortunately, he was killed resisting arrest, or we might have all been hanged.

But we had far more terrible concerns that evening than mere exposure of our lethal plot, for when we brought the President back to the White House, we found that he was still alive despite being shot directly in the head at close range with a large caliber pistol. Imagine our horror when the thing that the President had become opened his eyes and smiled at us. He seemed to know everything we had done, for he rose from couch upon which he had been placed and attacked

Seward. Such was the violence of the unexpected assault that he very nearly slew the Secretary of State before Phineas Gurley, the Chaplain of the Senate who had been summoned to pray for the President's soul, drew a strange object from his waistcoat that caused the demon animating the President to desist.

At Gurley's instruction, I slashed away the President's coat and shirt, revealing the terrible truth. The idol was embedded into the dead man's chest like a large, spiderish creature, the octopine tentacles pink and pulsing with parasitic life. It was with some difficulty that we managed to remove the demonic thing, being of course most careful not to touch it. At the very moment we pulled it from his flesh, the alien light faded from the President's eyes. It was the most peaceful I had seen him in months. I repent of my many sins and confess them freely as I prepare to meet my end, but the assassination of Abraham Lincoln was neither a sin nor an act for which I can repent. Had Lincoln lived, I am absolutely certain he would have become one of history's greatest monsters. Lincoln kept the Union together, but it was Seward who saved the nation from an evil far more terrible than either slavery or disunion.

I arranged for David Farragut to take the chest in which I secreted the idol on his next voyage across the Atlantic Ocean. Somewhere at sea, no one knows where, he weighted it with iron and dropped it into the depths. There, I believe, it will stay, forgotten until the end of time, its rapacious hunger for death unassuaged. You who read this, know there are evils lurking in the deep shadows of this world beyond the comprehension of men, and that it is ever the duty of those who are cursed to look into those shadows to remain vigilant against them.

Henry Halleck
Louisville, Kentucky
January 1, 1872

Once Our Land

As it happens, once our land
Was guaranteed the upper hand.
We ruled the seas from here to there
And landed armies everywhere.
The Kaiser, Hitler, Ho Chi Minh
No enemy could hope to win.
Our cities far from foreign shores,
Our people safe from far-off wars,
Grew fat in their security
From sea to ever-shining sea.

And so it was we thought to share
Our good fortune, as we could spare
The sacred seeds of liberty
Blooming on blood-watered tree.
We disregarded Europe's classes
And embraced the huddled masses
Come one, come all, out went the call
As hubris presages a fall,
For did not Man want to be free
And dwell in true equality?

German, Italian, Irish too,
Norwegian, Swedish, Dutch, and Jew,
They came to seek a better life

Escaping all that Old World strife.
And yet, they did not understand
The rights of every Englishman,
The Common Law was mystery
To grandchildren of serfs unfree.
And so they swore to flag and place
While seeking to transform the base.

Whatever happened, we had got
Atomic bombs, and they did not.
But then came Nineteen Sixty-Five
When sons of refugees contrived
To open doors to all the races
Black and brown and yellow faces.
Assuming our prosperity,
We gave away technology,
And ruined universities
While lauding our diversities.

God was dead, or so we heard,
And Nation just a racist word.
We learned a new and nobler Truth
Built on a dream of vibrant youth.
Our jobs went sailing overseas
And to incoming H1Bs.
When new genders invaded schools,
We realized that we'd been fools,
At last, we saw the dreadful fact
Of copybook gods coming back.

Once, we had the Maxim Gun
But these days, so does everyone.

So now we live in desperate times
And pay the price for history's crimes.

The Deported

It was the fourth day of our summer holiday in Vernazza, a little fishing village in the Cinque Terre. We had spent the morning on a charming hike through the hills, lunched in Monterosso al Mare, then enjoyed a languid afternoon in the sun on the beach there. After hiking back and taking a brief but restorative nap, the six of us had reconvened for the evening on the terrace overlooking the sea. We were well into our second bottle of prosecco as Francois attempted to convince Bertrand's wife, Michèle, that one could not genuinely claim to be an atheist and yet still believe in ghosts.

"There is more to a term than its etymology, *ma cherie*," he declared, punctuating his words with an authoritative jab of his cigarette. "When we reject the possibility of existence of gods, we are necessarily rejecting with it the very idea of the supernatural. If one cannot see it, or touch it, or experience it in any material manner, then it is entirely apparent that it simply does not exist."

"But what about love?" Michèle protested. She was an intelligent, educated woman, without a religious bone in her slender body, but she did harbor a lamentable affection for crystals, feng shui, and any number of fashionable absurdities. "What about hate?"

I reached out to place my glass on the side table when I noticed a smile on the face of the young German man sitting to our left. I had seen him before. He arrived in Vernazza the day after us, but apparently alone, for we had not seen him in the company of anyone other than the occasional waiter since then. He nodded to me, which I found to be a little surprising, as we had, of course, been speaking

French. The German, for such I naturally assumed him to be, was a big, beefy fellow, with a sun-reddened face and the sort of fine blond hair that is all too liable to disappear before a man's fortieth year.

"Pardon me, *monsieur*, I merely happened to overhear the conversation," he said in fluent, if provincial, French. "It reminded me of something."

"Ghosts or gods?" I asked him. The others, surprised to hear the German speaking our language, stopped talking and turned to listen to us.

"Perhaps both. Perhaps neither. Who can say?" He gave a shrug that was almost Gallic in its fatalism. "I only know there are things in this world that neither priest nor scientist can explain to my satisfaction. Things I have seen with my own eyes."

"Do you believe in God?" Bertrand leaned over and asked in an aggressive tone. He is one of my oldest and dearest friends, but at times, he can be a trial. He lost his beloved father at the age of seven in an automobile accident and has been demanding answers of God and anyone who is foolish enough to admit to believing in God ever since.

But the blond man only chuckled at his vehemence and raised his glass of red wine in an ironic salute. "I am Swiss. Of course I believe in God. Do we not worship Mammon?"

"Don't we all," Michèle said theatrically. Everyone laughed except Bertrand.

The Swiss's name was Beat Kistler. He was, he explained, from an old family in the canton of Zurich, but his mother was Vaudoise and he was awarded a criminology degree by the University of Lausanne. After graduation, he joined the Geneva police force and in his third year was reassigned to a task force assisting the Swiss Federal Migration Office in processing immigrants who were seeking asylum. And it was there, in the detention center, that he had seen something that he found inexplicable, even now. We were all interested to hear his mysterious story, for it was eminently clear that he was an educated and level-headed man. He told us his tale without resort to drama, in a calm and relaxed manner.

"The first thing you must understand," he said, "is that most of the asylum seekers we see in the federal system are Africans. Nigerians are the most common. They're economic migrants, of course, but somewhere along the way, word gets around the community that if they can present themselves as political victims, there is a chance they will be able to receive a residence permit and stay in the country. We can't allow most of them to remain, you understand, because they have no skills, they have no means of supporting themselves, and they simply cannot afford to live in such an expensive country. The franc is very high, you know. And, in any event, we have no room for them; there literally isn't anywhere for them to live. The city of Lagos alone has more people than we have in all of Switzerland.

"The Migration Office reviews about fifteen thousand applicants per year. About a third of them can be sent immediately to other European states, because the Dublin accord requires them to apply for asylum in the state that served as their port of entry. So we send them to Italy, Spain, or in some cases, to you, in France. Another third leave on their own once we explain to them that they will not, under any circumstances, be permitted to remain. But the remainder —ah, well, that is where things occasionally get out of order.

"You should hear the lies they tell. Many times, they are most amusing. The sort of young men who are adventurous enough to make it all the way to Switzerland from Africa seldom have much in the way of education and so it's not uncommon for them to fail to properly understand what their legal advisers are telling them to say. So we hear men claiming they are facing female genital mutilation should they be forced to return home, or telling us their entire family was killed in a massacre even though we already have the rejected applications from three of their brothers in our files. Occasionally a story will check out and permission will be granted, but only in the most extreme cases. Out of the two thousand Nigerians who applied last year, I think perhaps one or two were given residence. The rest, we must somehow transport back to their home country."

"Only one or two?" my wife protested. "Out of thousands? Surely you could take more!"

Beat smiled and shook his head. "A fifth of our residents are already foreigners as it is. And recall, none of these people are being oppressed or tortured in any way, in which case we would have a moral duty to help them. They simply want to live off the Swiss people. It's not possible."

"Enough about the Africans, what about the ghosts!" Bertrand was getting impatient.

"Before you can understand the significance of this, my friends, you must first accept the context of the situation. But I see that you have grasped the general idea, therefore I shall move on to the specific case of which I speak.

"Two years ago, I met a Nigerian man who did not fit the description of the sort of asylum seekers we are accustomed to see every day. He was older, in his fifties, and instead of giving his religion as either Christian or Muslim, his file showed that he was classified as an animist. The traditional religions are officially recognized in Nigeria, and in fact many of those who call themselves Christians or Muslims still pay due regard to their tribal gods and ancestral spirits.

"I was tasked to accompany the social worker who was assigned to interview him for his appeal hearing. This was necessary because both the asylum seekers and the deportees are held in detainment facilities, and, like prisoners everywhere, they sometimes get unruly. It's mostly those who have already been sentenced to deportation, since they have little to lose if they behave badly, but sometimes the asylum seekers forget themselves and get out of hand as well.

"The contrast between the facilities and the inhabitants is stark. It is literally black and white. Most of the facilities are very new, all squares and fluorescent lighting, with undecorated walls painted white and the ceilings and floors covered with white tile. You cannot imagine a more lifeless and sterile environment. The Nigerians, on the other hand, are very dark-skinned and full of life. When they are happy, they sing and smile, and some of them play a sort of rhythmic music with their hands on the walls to which the others dance. Of course, some of them, particularly the less intelligent, are demoralized by their incarceration. In such cases, their behavior at times borders on the bestial. They glare and they snarl, they beg and they plead, at times they offer their bodies for pleasure, other times they spit at anyone who walks past their cells.

"This man was not one of the ones who act like animals. He had a dignity to him, and his file showed he had been a man of some substance in Lagos. His brother, now deceased, was a senior official in the Ministry of Finance, but he was closely tied to the progressive opposition party, which accounted for his emigration from the country after the corrupt election of 2007 that was essentially stolen by the party in power today.

"He spoke English; better English than I do. When the social worker interviewed him, he explained in a very lucid and coherent manner that to return to Nigeria meant death, not only for him, but for everyone around him. The reason he gave was that he had been cursed by an Igbo shaman in the employ of the new finance minister, the same man who was responsible for his brother's death. He told us he was a shaman himself, but his ancestral spirits had been defeated by the shaman's spirits during the conflict that surrounded the election in 2007."

Michèle and I laughed. Bertrand snorted. "How did the immigration judge view that?"

"The social worker tried several times to explain to him that his appeal would be rejected, as ancestral spirits are not listed among the potential justifications for asylum accepted by the foreign office, but the Nigerian was absolutely insistent. He said he would not lie and he was absolutely convinced that his return would prove fatal, because the Igbo spirits would not permit it. As I said, he was a serious and dignified man. If his claim hadn't been so clearly impossible, one might have almost found it to 'be persuasive.

"I don't know if the social worker actually cited the spirits or how things went at the hearing, all I know is that the appeal was unsuccessful, which of course was hardly surprising. The whole incident was very strange, but at the time I thought nothing more of it until two months later, when my entire unit was summoned in the middle of the night to help the Securitas guards deal with a riot that had broken out at that very facility. We were sent in wearing full riot gear, although we were only armed with mace and batons. We left our shields in the bus they used to bring us there, since they would only get in the way."

"You must have been very frightened," interjected Aurélie, Francois's partner of the last five years.

"No, for the most part we were annoyed at being dragged from the comfort of our beds. A few of the more aggressive lads, they were bragging about how they were going to break heads and so forth, you know the type. But mostly we only wanted to go in, get the job done, and hopefully return in time to get a few hours of sleep before the sun came up. I'd been on duty since the morning at the federal court in Bern, so my main sentiment was one of exhaustion.

"Once we entered, however, we quickly realized it wasn't a riot. All the lights were out, but the facility technicians said there was no loss of power, which was confusing. Our helmets have flashlights, so we switched them on and entered. There was screaming, but they were screams of terror, not the wordless roaring you hear when a crowd is out of control, and they were coming from somewhere deep inside the building. The asylum seekers were still in their cells, but most of the deportees were gathered in the cafeteria and out of their heads with fear. They weren't rioting; they'd broken out of their cells because they were all scared to death of something. They greeted us with hugs and tears, as if we were their saviors. Right about then, the screams stopped. I think the sudden silence, more than anything else, started to make us feel nervous.

"Our captain talked one of them, a big man with a shaved head, into leading us towards the deportee cells from where the screams had been coming. Most of the cells were empty, but then we came upon a cell with a closed door. The captain had the keys, so he unlocked it and discovered two dead Nigerians inside. Their eyes were open, but they were dead and there wasn't a mark on them. The deportee who was acting as our guide was shaking a little, but he said he was a Jesus man and 'the shadow that kill' couldn't touch him. We passed two more locked cells and found a pair of dead Nigerians inside both of them, and again, the dead men were unmarked.

"Now remember, it was pitch black down there, except for our helmet lights, which aren't as powerful as they should be. I thought I heard something, so I took my baton out, shook it out to its full length, and went to investigate. I looked in a cell on the other side of the hall, and first things I saw were two eyes; big, round, white eyes, almost like when your automobile catches a fox's eyes along the side of the road. Then I saw the rest of it…

"I must have shouted because there were eight or nine lights shining into the cell almost right away."

"The old man, the shaman—" breathed Francois.

"Precisely," nodded the Swiss. "He was crouched over the body of his cellmate, eating his heart! It was the murdered man we had heard screaming earlier, the cellmate. The shaman had painted all sorts of evil-looking symbols on the walls of their cell in his blood, before finally taking his heart and killing him. He must have been at it for an hour or more, because the floor was completely covered in blood. When they counted later, there were more than one hundred separate symbols on the walls."

"What did the symbols mean?"

"The psychologists asked him that later. We didn't ask questions then, you see, we just unlocked the cell, threw open the door, maced him and put him in shackles. There wasn't anything we could do for the cellmate, of course. But the symbols; that's the intriguing thing. He told the psychologists they were to summon the spirits of the Igbo ancestors and offer them the lives of the men in the cells around him as an attempt to appease them. He said the six men who died in the other cells meant that his offering had been accepted, but it was all to no avail since we had interrupted him before he could finish the ritual. His cellmate was Igbo, so that's why he had to eat his heart; to sort of make himself Igbo, in a way, so the spirits would see him as one of theirs and leave him alone when he returned to Lagos."

"That sounds rather heartless of the man," Bertrand commented wryly.

"Bertrand!" Michèle protested. "But didn't you say you had to unlock his cell when you found him?"

"It was locked. So were the other cells. But the other men were definitely dead as well and the times of their deaths were found to be consistent with the time that the lights went out and the riot started."

"Interesting," mused Bertrand. "Of course, these other Nigerians were uneducated, superstitious, and more or less animists for the most part. Therefore, it is safe to assume they were highly susceptible to suggestion. You said that even the Christian man was terrified. So, if they knew he was a shaman and became aware of what he intended, it's entirely possible that they were quite literally frightened to death!"

"But that doesn't explain the lights," I pointed out.

"That might have merely been an unfortunate coincidence."

"Be that as it may, the lights came on a few minutes after we maced the shaman," the Swiss explained. "But that's not the end of my story. Three months after the riot, my friend Walther and I were assigned to the squad that accompanies the deportation flight to Lagos. When we reviewed the deportee list, I recognized one of the names as belonging to the man I'd last seen devouring his companion's heart. I will not lie; at that moment I felt such a fear as I have never known before. I heard no voice, but suddenly I understood the message, as clearly as you hear me speak to you now, that I should not, under any circumstances, board that flight. The ancestral spirits were strong enough to kill six healthy young men a continent away—and the ritual meant to appease them had been a failure.

"I made some excuse to my captain, told him I was unwell or something, I don't recall. To my shame, I did not do more than make a half-hearted attempt to convince Walther to avoid the flight as well. I arranged to have lunch with him, but when I mentioned my fears, he laughed at me for being an irrational, superstitious fool and I was too embarrassed to argue the point with him. I bitterly regretted that a week later, when I received a telephone call from my captain. He told me that the Swiss flight from Zurich to Lagos had gone down not long after entering Nigerian airspace. There were no survivors."

"Oh my God," breathed Michèle.

"How awful for you," said my wife.

The Swiss only smiled ruefully and lit a cigarette. He inhaled thoughtfully, and tapped out the small amount of ash on the tip. "Rather more awful for Walther and the others, I should think."

"What caused the crash?" I asked. "I can't imagine the aviation authorities attributed it to angry ancestral spirits."

"After the black box was analyzed, the experts concluded that the co-pilot had fallen asleep and the pilot had a heart attack. But to my mind, that sounds like an attempt to explain away the inexplicable. There was no mechanical failure and no suggestion of distress in the cockpit. Unfortunately the plane burned, so conjecture was all that was left to them in the absence of anything conclusive from the black box."

He looked at Bertrand. "So, have you an explanation for me, other than an unfortunate string of unlikely coincidences?"

Bertrand, to his credit, wasn't inclined to bluster. "I fear you have anticipated me, *monsieur*. Of course, I am hardly an expert on aviation."

We were all quick to protest the idea that Bertrand might be anything less than expert on everything. It was an old joke among us. Amidst the laughter, the Swiss extinguished his cigarette and rose from his chair.

"Ladies, gentlemen, I bid you *une bonne soirée* and a pleasant remainder to your vacation. And I hope my little tale has not disturbed you."

Bertrand and I hastened to assure him that it was impossible, as we had enjoyed it immensely. Were we not all *français*, hailing from the most rational of nations? We bade him farewell, and the last we saw of him was his broad back, as he returned to the bar inside.

Later that evening, as my wife slept by my side, there was a soft knock on my door. It was Bertrand, and he was holding his iPad. "Come outside and look at this," he whispered.

I followed him out to the patio where we had been drinking earlier that evening. We could hear the sound of the sea below us, but where there had been a broad expanse of clear blue water only a few hours before, there was now nothing but a vast black emptiness, devoid of reflections from the shore or even the pinpricks of starlight that animated the night sky above. The glow of the tablet screen was so bright against the darkness that it was almost painful to my eyes. And what had been unthinkable under the warm glow of the Italian sun suddenly seemed all too possible, when standing above the inky abyss of the Mediterranean at midnight.

"I looked it up. A flight from Zurich to Lagos that was carrying twenty deportees, eight police, and the two pilots went down about eighteen months ago."

"So that much was true, anyhow."

We stared out at the black depths of the sea. It was a quiet evening and the Moon was obscured by clouds that had crept in under the cover of darkness. The waves lapped at the rocky shoreline hundreds of meters below us, indifferent, mindless, uncaring, exactly as they had one thousand, two thousand, three thousand years ago.

"This doesn't prove anything about the existence of ghosts, much less God," Bertrand suddenly declared.

"Of course not," I said. "But still…"

"But still," he agreed.

Bane Walks On

He stalked into the shadowed vale
His six-gun at his side,
A twelve-gauge strapped across his back
And boots with knives inside.

He spared no glance for lives behind
Nor for the lurking dark
That shivered as he passed it by,
Eyes ever cold and stark.

A shrouded wight stood in his way,
Its bony hand did twitch
White-knuckled on its wicked scythe.
"Not you, son of a bitch!"

The tall man only grinned and told
His foe to go to Hell.
The Reaper bowed and stepped aside,
A past lesson learned well.

Beyond the darkness, blinding light
Caused his hard eyes to narrow.
And still the man stood tall and proud
His back straight as an arrow.

Then thunder roared high overhead.
"My son, you're here at last!"
Fear not, I have much work for you
A labor long and vast.

"I am the God of Grace and yet
There must be Justice too.
I hear the cries of the despised
The wicked owe their due.

"Some serve with harps and sing My praise,
Hosannas with each breath.
But you shall sing a different song,
My new Angel of Death."

The tall man kneeled and bowed his head.
"Lord, I shall do Your Will."
And then he smiled, baring his teeth,
"Just tell me who to kill."

Seven Kill Tiger

Zhang Zedong stared at his screen in disbelief. The monthly production numbers had fallen again, down from the previous quarter's low that had already led to one alarmingly polite video call from the Vice-Chairman of the Central Military Commission. General Xu was not technically in his formal chain of command, but as the largest individual shareholder in the China African Industries Group, the general's opinion was of considerably more concern to Zhang than that of his immediate superior, the Executive Vice-President for East Africa.

The damned *hei ren* were going to get him replaced, he thought bitterly. If he was fortunate. In the event General Xu decided that the growing gap between the region's quarterly objectives and the actual results achieved was the consequence of excessive greed rather than Zhang's inability to make the natives work, his family would be receiving a bill for the price of the bullet used to execute him before long.

But he hadn't diverted any significant resources into his own pockets, not any more than was expected of an executive in his position. He didn't have more than eleven or twelve million dollars safely stashed away in his American bank accounts, and if his son was studying at the University of California, Berkeley, so were fifty other children of high-ranking Party members. Still, it would be enough to see him shot if the general was looking for an excuse.

What he needed was more reliable workers. What he needed was more Han people. In Zambia alone, there were now 750,000 Chinese living in what amounted to a small colonial city, but they lived in walled enclaves almost under siege from the thieves, robbers, and rapists who preyed upon them daily despite the best efforts of CAIG's security forces to protect them. The police were useless, worse than useless, actually, as they were often among the worst thieves and sexual predators of all.

He sighed. Africa would be a glorious place were it not for the Africans. He'd been warned before coming to Lusaka that ninety percent of the *hei ren* were thieves, but he discounted that warning as the customary Han superiority complex. After seven years of futility in attempting to turn CAIG's $35 billion investment in the country into something resembling a reasonable return, he was beginning to wonder if that estimate had been on the low side.

Lusaka had always been known for its crime, but of late the criminal gangs were getting bolder. Just last week, ten young hei ren armed with AK-47s shot dead the two African security guards outside a gated Chinese complex, raped four young Chinese girls, and kidnapped two mining company executives. The company had paid the ransoms, which were trivial, and gotten its executives back, but the fear and outrage in the business community was palpable. Then, to make matters even worse, one of the girls committed suicide in shame at having been violated by *hóuzi*, and now the hunger for revenge in the expat community was threatening to get out of control.

To absolutely no one's surprise, the local police proved unable to identify the perpetrators, let alone arrest them. As far as Zhang could tell, they genuinely had no idea which of the eight gangs actively operating in the city might have been responsible.

If only the National People's Congress had followed through on its original plan to send 100 million colonists to Africa! But that plan had met with intense international criticism, and it wouldn't necessarily be enough anyhow; the problem wasn't limited to the dearth of Han labor. Bringing in more proper workers would solve the production problem, but it wouldn't solve the crime problem or the growing fraternization problem either. Far too many Chinese girls had fallen for the blandishments of persistent African suitors, failing to understand why the locals had so much time to pursue them or realize that the liaisons were unlikely to go anywhere in the long term. Even on the rare occasions a marriage did come to pass, what resulted was seldom what the average Chinese girl understood to be marriage.

African men thought of themselves as lions, and they lived like kings of beasts, entirely content to lounge about living off the labor of one or more of his lionesses. And the girls who succumbed to their exotic appeal could not return to China, not those who bore half-African bastards anyway. It was a growing problem, and even if it wasn't Zhang's responsibility, as CAIG's Senior Vice-President and Director for Zambia, Zimbabwe, Mozambique, and Tanzania, there were many looking to him to find a solution. But what was he supposed to do, ban interracial relations? Temporarily sterilize every Chinese woman between the ages of 10 and 40? Forbid Chinese firms to hire locals for even the most menial jobs? Any action that might make a substantive difference would generate a hailstorm of international protest that would focus very unwanted attention on him from General Xu, and perhaps even the Central Commission.

What he needed, he decided, was new ideas. Everything he had tried to date had failed. Positive incentives, negative incentives, threats, bribes, and shouting, everything had failed. The Americans had a curious phrase he'd heard once on a visit to California, the "Come to Jesus" meeting. He didn't quite grasp what it meant, exactly, but he decided it would serve as his inspiration for the staff meeting he intended to call tomorrow morning. Because if they didn't come up with something that at least had the potential to lead the way out of this utter debacle, he fully intended to rain fire and brimstone down upon them all.

He might not be able to avoid going down himself, but he could damn well ensure that he didn't go down alone.

Philip Thompson was reading a report of a small measles outbreak in Ecuador when a knock on the open door to his office disturbed him. He looked up and saw it was Scott Berens, one of his junior analysts, standing in the doorway.

"You heard about Ecuador, Dr. Thompson?" the younger man asked.

"Reading about it now. Looks as if the government has it under control."

"They caught it early enough. It's the Tungurahua province again. That's been a problem area for the Ministry of Health since 1996. The vaccination program misses too many of the indigenous children."

"Understandable." Thompson put the report down on his desk. "What's on your mind, Scott?"

"Do you remember that unknown outbreak in northern Zambia we started tracking six months ago?"

"I thought that was a false alarm."

"It was, insofar as we were able to determine that it wasn't Ebola, which was the initial concern. And there were only 142 cases and 26 deaths before it burned itself out, so we didn't even bother sending anyone over to investigate."

Thompson clicked his tongue against his lower lip, wondering where Berens was going with this. The young man was a bright young doctor and had graduated in the top ten percent of his class from Johns Hopkins, so he assumed Berens must have a good reason for bringing such an obscure incident to his attention.

"Are you saying we should have?"

"No, it's just that I was reading over the statistics, as part of a paper I was thinking about writing on east Africa, when I noticed an anomaly."

"What's that?"

"The population of the nearest town. It's mostly Chinese. I think they have a big mining camp up there."

Thompson shrugged and spread his hands. "It's hardly a secret that China has been moving into Africa in a big way for the last two decades. They have hundreds of such towns."

"True, but that only explains why the Chinese were there. It doesn't explain why most of the cases, and all of the deaths, were African. Only five Chinese were affected and all five recovered. Beyond the basic statistical odds involved, you would think the native population would be more resistantto whatever virus makes its way out of the jungle, not more susceptible to it."

Thompson frowned. Berens was right. It was an anomaly. And if there was one thing he had learned after 22 years at the Centers for Disease Control, it was to pay particular attention to anomalies.

"Good catch, Scott. Dig into it and see if it's really just a mining town or if the PLA happens to have any laboratories or science facilities in the area. Not necessarily where the outbreak took place, but anywhere in the surrounding area. They went dark on the bio-war front a few years ago, and it may be that some of their test facilities were moved from Xi'an to Africa. This just might give us some insight as to where they went."

"Do you think someone got careless and a bio-weapon escaped the lab, Dr. Thompson?" There was an eager glint in the younger man's eyes that made Thompson smile despite himself. Such a discovery, even if it was never published in any of the public journals, could be the making of Berens's career, and both of them knew it.

"Let's not get ahead of ourselves, Scott. Go and see what you can find about this mining town, what is it called?"

"Mpolokoso."

"Right." He didn't even bother trying to pronounce it. "Look into what the Chinese are doing there and we'll see if it could have any connection to this mysterious outbreak. Write it up and email it to me; I'll call you when I've had a chance to read it and think it over."

"Will do, Dr. Thompson!" Berens made a mock salute with the paper and disappeared from the doorway.

Thompson leaned back in his chair, reflecting on the unwelcome news. Unlike his young subordinate, he already knew they weren't likely to find any evidence of laboratories, research facilities, an escaped bio-weapon, or even anything that was conventionally considered to be a bio-weapon. Conventional bio-weapons didn't discriminate between Asian and Sub-Saharan haplogroups. Genetic weapons, on the other hand, were designed to do just that. And he very much doubted that whatever it was had been released accidentally.

After consulting his contact list, he tapped in the number for Fort Detrick. A young enlisted woman answered the phone.

"US-AMRIID. How may I direct your call?"

"This is Dr. Phil Thompson of the CDC. Get me Colonel Hill, please."

"Right away, sir." She paused. "The CDC... is this urgent, sir?"

He smiled grimly. "That's exactly what I'm trying to determine."

It was the massacre that convinced Zhang to take action. After a Chinese entrepreneur's young daughter in Kapiri Mposhi was raped and killed by a pair of copper miners, the man took his vengeance by tracking the perpetrators down and shooting them dead at the New Kapira Mphoshi railway station. The shootings were caught on closed-circuit television, and before Zhang or anyone in Lusaka even knew about the incident, the images had spread all over Zambia and Tanzania, inflaming the African community, and in particular, the Nyanja-Chewa tribe to which the two miners belonged.

Within a week, all 87 Chinese residents of Kapiri Mposhi were dead. Some had been shot, some had been necklaced, but most had fallen to the knives of the Nyau, a masked secret society known for black magic and channeling the spirits of the dead. The pictures were horrific. Zhang stared at them for a long time.

Black magic. I will show them black magic. I will show them their worst nightmares!

The Kapiri Mposhi massacre had been six months ago. Now the time to unleash the spirits of righteous vengeance had very nearly come, Zhang thought, as a tall young scientist entered his office. Gao Xing was humble and diffident. Despite his height, he could have walked down the street in Weinan or Xi'an without anyone taking notice of him. Only his eyes gave any sign that he might be unusual. They were coldly arrogant, and conveyed little in the way of warmth or humanity. He was in his middle twenties, and his pale skin indicated that he spent very little time outside under the Zambian sun.

The perfect scientist, Zhang thought wryly. The poor kid had probably never had a girlfriend. But the young girl in Kapiri Mposhi, the very first one to die, had been his cousin. He might not know how to love, but assuredly, he knew how to hate.

"They tell me your most recent test of Huáng Hu was successful."

"Yes, Director. The terminal rate is now in excess of 80 percent. Based on the most conservative spread models, the pseudo-epidemic will cross the Angolan border within two weeks. Within nine months, the continent is expected to be clear of all undesirable populations. The task of disposal will obviously be enormous, and will create considerable additional health hazards, but I would expect that it would be safe to begin the settlement programs within 18 months of zero day."

"Zero day?"

"The date upon which any opposing forces will be unable to stop the virus from going terminal in the target population. The estimates vary, but the average indicates zero day is D-day plus 28."

"Is there any way to reduce the time to zero day?"

"Increase the number of transmission vectors, preferably in a manner scattered widely across the continent."

Zhang nodded. "I will think on that."

"If I may offer a suggestion, Director?"

"Please do."

"There is an American foundation that has malaria vaccination campaigns running in every country in Africa. If a way could be found to substitute the substances injected, zero day could be reduced to a matter of two weeks or less."

"Wouldn't that increase the risk of detection?"

"Certainly." The young scientist's dark eyes were unperturbed. "But in light of how the vaccination campaigns are already regarded with a significant amount of local suspicion, detection would likely sow sufficient confusion to inhibit any effective response. Especially because the NGOs tasked with the response would be widely regarded as the guilty parties."

"And combined with cutting the potential response time in half, it's almost surely worth the risk as long as the substitutions can be made undetected."

"I cannot speak to that, Director. It is outside my competence."

Zhang thought a moment. "It's too risky to interfere with the Americans. We don't know their protocols. But Sinovac has a polio vaccine that's already been prequalified by the World Health Organization and the Global Polio Eradication Initiative has endorsed it as a substitute for their primary oral vaccine. It would be much easier to substitute that. We can even arrange to have the vaccines shipped in through Dar es Salaam."

"As you say, Director."

Zhang couldn't help but smile. The young scientist could not have made his indifference to anything but the technical aspects related to his specialty any more clear. "The potential consequences do not trouble you, Dr. Gao?"

"Not in the slightest, Director Zhang. To the contrary, you have my deepest admiration. What you propose to accomplish will make the Great Leap Forward appear little more than a precursor to the true advancement. What began as a Cultural Revolution has become a Scientific Revolution. Soon China will stand astride the globe as the master of two continents, and the nations of the world will bow before her!"

Zhang found himself mildly appalled by the young man's fanaticism. Did Mao ever feel similarly alarmed by the enthusiasm of his own Red Guards? But the sentiments Gao expressed were sound enough. Africa was wasted on the Africans. China had spent 50 million Chinese lives to become a 20th-century power, how could she hesitate to spend twenty times that many more African lives to assume her rightful place as the one true 21st-century superpower?

"Thank you, Dr. Gao."

"Director." The young man bowed and left his office.

Zhang reflected on Gao's words. A Scientific Revolution. A Greater Leap Forward! The young scientist's confidence in the project quelled any remaining doubts that it was time to move forward and let the Central Military Commission know about his plans for the Dark Continent. But one question still remained: to release Huáng Hu before or after General Xu's scheduled visit?

It would be a shame, after all, if he were to be executed before releasing the spirits to seek their revenge.

The World Health Organization (WHO) has announced the prequalification of a Chinese-made vaccine for polio. The new WHO pre-qualified vaccine is produced by Sinovac Biotech Ltd, and is an inactive-virus vaccine that is considered to be safer than the live-virus vaccines now widely used across Asia and Africa.

"WHO prequalification of the Sinovac vaccine is another feather in the cap of China's growing vaccine manufacturing industry," said Dr. Bernhard Schwartländer, WHO Representative in China.

"This is also very good news for the millions of children in low- and middle-income countries which cannot afford to manufacture or purchase their inactive-virus vaccines. WHO prequalification of Sinovac's vaccine will add to the worldwide arsenal of anti-polio vaccines, assisting the global campaign to eradicate the disease. In doing so, it will help to save lives," Dr. Schwartländer said. "Sinovac's polio vaccine is the second vaccine made in China to achieve WHO prequalification, following prequalification of a Japanese-made encephalitis vaccine in 2013 and Hualan Biological's influenza vaccine in 2015."

Philip Thompson shook his head as he returned the printout to Scott Berens. "You don't seriously imagine that the Chinese would use a weaponized vaccine as a vehicle for genetic warfare, do you? They could maybe get one hot lot into the distribution system, two at most, and I can't imagine that could possibly be worth permanently trashing their ability to access the export markets!"

"No, of course not." His subordinate shrugged "You told me to dig up anything that might be related to possible launch vectors. This is the only one I found that could conceivably be connected to Chinese corporate activity in the last two years."

"I'd use bird flu myself," Thompson mused.

"What's that?"

"If you're going to weaponize something, an aerosol vector is the most effective. And the world is accustomed to bird flu coming out of China every few years. That's what that vaccine from Hualan was, it was an H1N1 vaccine. You could even combine the two, put the bomb in the flu virus itself, then trigger it with the vaccine."

"Now who is imagining things, Doctor?"

Thompson smiled. "Well, perhaps it's nothing after all. There haven't been any further outbreaks in the last six months, so I suppose it was simply another unknown jungle disease. Here is hoping we've seen the last of it."

General Xu stood staring motionless at the image of the continent of Africa on the screen, his hands clasped behind his back, his square face impassive and unreadable. Zhang watched the man closely, looking for some sign of approval, of anger, of anything that would give him some indication of his fate. Finally, the general turned to face him, and something in the soldier's eyes seemed to indicate that he was feeling powerful emotion.

To Zhang's utter astonishment, the general bowed to him, so deeply that his torso was nearly parallel to the floor. Zhang didn't know what to do; he just stood there respectfully and hoped that the general's action was a good sign.

"You are a man of rare vision and a great tribute to our race," General Xu said hoarsely. "Not since Da Duo Shou himself has China been blessed with a man of such insight! You have broken the power of the gun that has kept us chained since the *yingguo ren* arrived! You have abolished war with science!"

"The General is not displeased?"

The general indicated the screen. "Far from it. Your proposal is promising, extremely promising, Director. I will go to Beijing immediately and consult with the Chairman. How soon can you begin?"

"Three weeks. The next shipment from Sinovac will arrive in ten days. I am told it will take four days to replace the vaccines and reseal the vials. Then we will need to distribute them to the aid offices. We will start the flu-based vector in Mozambique two weeks prior to the first inoculations. Even if the Americans or the Europeans somehow manage to react quickly to one attack, the very effort required to do so will inhibit their ability to respond to the other."

"Remarkable!" The general shook his head admiringly. "Director, surely you were inspired by your ancestors! What led you to conceive such a vision?"

"Once all struggle is grasped, miracles are possible."

"Well said. What is the name of this miracle?"

"Huáng Hu."

General Xu was an educated man. He smiled. "How very appropriate, Director. I shall inform you of the Chairman's decision before the end of the week. You will launch the initial phase on his command."

Zhang bowed, feeling both triumph and relief. It seemed he would survive the day. And the restless ghosts of Kapiri Mposhi would be avenged, a thousandfold and more. "Thank you, General."

As his Prius moved silently through the Georgia night, Philip Thompson thought about what he'd learned from his conversation earlier that day with Colonel Hill. He didn't know how to feel about the information he was trying to process. Far from being unthinkable, it was apparent to anyone capable of reading between the lines that the U.S. Army had already developed genetic weapons very similar to those he'd adduced the Chinese were developing. Moreover, the Russian Army and the IDF were well along the process of doing the same.

It was madness. Sheer madness. The world's militaries were quite literally preparing—prepared—to undo everything that Man's most dedicated warriors against the dread Rider on the Pale Horse had ever accomplished. The painstaking labor of decades could be undone in a matter of hours, and with a genocidal precision that had hitherto been literally unimaginable. Even though he'd known the United States could not permit itself to fall behind in such an important technological aspect of war, it was shattering to know, to actually have it confirmed beyond any shadow of a doubt, that his own government was preparing to exterminate entire populations. It was possible. There was no defense, as such. There was only deterrence. Or, perhaps, revenge.

How are we any better than them? The thought of warring genocides sickened him, all the more so knowing that he and all of his colleagues would be the first to be drafted and put on the front lines— the front labs—if any such genetic war should erupt. He was a doctor, he was a scientist, he was a healer. He had gone into medicine, and after that, science, in order to help people, not to kill them on an industrial scale!

And the worst thing was that he could not unburden his soul to anyone; the colonel had let him know, in no uncertain terms, that if he so much breathed a word of what he had learned to anyone else at the CDC, let alone the press, he would be prosecuted for violating national security.

The garage door recognized his license plate and opened automatically as he approached. He parked the car, took his briefcase from the passenger seat, and walked through the parking garage to the elevator. His apartment was on the fifth floor, and there was an audible snick as the door's face-scanner recognized him and unlocked the door. But he stopped in the doorway after opening the door: there was a soft glow from the living room indicating that one of the lights was on.

That was strange. He worked late so often that he was always careful to make sure the lights were all out before he left in the morning, so as not to waste electricity. Then he shrugged and closed the door behind him. He'd had a lot on his mind recently and must have forgotten to turn one of them off.

But when he walked down the hallway and turned the corner, he froze. An Asian man dressed all in black was sitting in his recliner, legs crossed, casually perusing the previous month's issue of *Nature*.

"Good evening. Have a seat, Dr. Thompson." The intruder indicated the couch to his right. He spoke perfect, unaccented English.

Dumbfounded and frightened, Philip obeyed. What are you doing here, he wanted to demand, but he was afraid that he already knew the answer. Did the man have a gun? He probably did. Was it worth trying to make a break for one of the knives in the kitchen? No, almost certainly not.

"You needn't be alarmed, Dr. Thompson. I realize this is unsettling, but please understand that I'm not here to harm you."

Philip swallowed hard, then couldn't help exhaling heavily with sudden relief. He hadn't even realized he was holding his breath. "Why… why are you here?"

The intruder smiled, flashing straight white teeth. Probably not Japanese. Chinese-American? "I am here to encourage you to take that vacation in Hawaii. According to your calendar, it begins tomorrow. Fourteen days on Maui, at the Grand Wailea. It's about time you used up some of that vacation time you've been hoarding, after all."

"Hawaii? I don't have a vacation—"

"Ah, but you do!" The Asian man produced a folder and withdrew airplane tickets and an itinerary before sliding them across the coffee table to Philip. "If you check your emails, you'll see that you requested a vacation three months ago and it was approved by Deputy Director Sansom back in May."

"You hacked the CDC computers?"

"Dr. Thompson, with all due respect, we've been privy to all of your communications with Colonel Hill and everyone else at AMRIID for months. Making a few modifications to your email server is about as difficult as changing an undergraduate's grades at Georgia Tech."

"What do you expect me to do?"

"Take the vacation. And then, when they fly you to Frederick, do your job. Analyze the virus and tell them the truth about it."

"The truth. What is that?"

"The fact that the virus is no threat at all to 98 percent of the American population. Aside from some recent immigrants, most of whom are not American citizens anyway, your people will be entirely unaffected."

Philip sat back, his mind racing, rapidly putting together the various facts at his disposal. It was obvious that the man was a Chinese intelligence agent. Then he gasped. "Dear God! Is your government intending to murder the entire sub-Saharan population? That's over one billion people!"

"I have no idea, Dr. Thompson. We can speculate if you like, but I imagine you probably know more about it than I do. My part in this ends tonight, whereas you still have a very important role to play. In fact, one might go so far as to say the fate of the entire human race is in your hands. That's why I am here speaking to you now. It is possible that you will be all that stands in the way of a third world war."

Still reeling from the horrific conclusion he'd reached, Philip could only shake his head. Mass murder? The human race in his hands? World War III?

"When the news of the virus breaks, there will be widespread fear throughout your government hierarchy. Even panic. It is very important that someone with sufficient stature and the ability to understand exactly what is happening will be in a position to tell your President, and his generals, that there is no serious threat to America. My superiors do not wish to see a necessary evil transformed into an unnecessary apocalypse. Neither a genetic war nor a nuclear war between China and the United States will serve anyone's interests, as I'm sure you will admit."

"Retaliation," Philip murmured. "You want me to tell them not to retaliate."

"I expect you to tell them that retaliation would be tantamount to mutual suicide," the agent corrected. "As is, in fact, the case. As I said, we simply want you to enjoy your vacation, then do your job and tell them the truth. Nothing more than the truth. It is well within your competence."

"I assume that if I don't keep my mouth shut about what you are intending, you will kill me."

The agent smiled regretfully and gave a slight nod. "We are, of course, monitoring you very closely. If you attempt to communicate with anyone—anyone—then I fear it is very likely that a disgruntled former employee will return to the CDC with a pair of inexpensive handguns and kill a number of people there, yourself included, before committing suicide."

He withdrew another piece of paper from his folder and slid it across to Philip. It was a color printout with ten photographs, driver's licenses by the looks of them, and each one was familiar to Philip. Two former girlfriends, two more casual liaisons, and six of the nine other members of his fantasy football league. All of them were friends, all of them were people he cared about.

Philip snorted bitterly and shook his head. The ruthless bastards certainly did their homework. He'd all but forgotten about the weekend fling with Caitlin five years ago. She was married to a banker now, with a baby at home and another on the way.

"You cannot prevent what is about to happen, Dr. Thompson. But you can stop an even greater horror from taking place. You cannot save the Africans, but you can save the rest of the human race."

The Chinese agent extended the folder in his gloved hand. Philip took it, then returned the sheet with the pictures on it, but retained the tickets.

"Very wise, Dr. Thompson."

"Can I ask you one question?"

For the first time, the agent looked surprised, but he nodded.

"How on Earth do you people sleep at night?"

The agent laughed, genuinely amused.

"Soundly, in the knowledge that we are serving our nation, Doctor. We sleep very soundly indeed."

The message from the Chairman of the Central Military Commission was a short one that consisted of only four ideographs. It seemed the Chairman, too, was an educated man. Zhang nodded solemnly to Dr. Gao, who peered at the screen in confusion.

"This means we are to proceed? 'Heaven births ten thousand things'? I don't understand. What does it mean, Director?"

"It means we are ordered to release Huáng Hu," Zhang said calmly. "Dr. Gao, please initiate the procedure to release the Yellow Tiger."

Heaven brings forth innumerable things to nurture man.
Man has nothing good with which to recompense Heaven.
Kill. Kill. Kill. Kill. Kill. Kill. Kill.

Shinjuku Satan

They call me doctor. Partly because I have a doctorate in neuropsychology from Nanyang Technopolitan, but mostly because doctor is what you call the man in the white coat when you, or your kid, or your cat, isn't feeling well. Most of the time, the doctor can fix what's wrong with you, the kid, or the cat. And when he can't, then the doctor is the guy who gets called in to put them down.

I have an office on the 40th floor of the Tanjong Pagar Center, but it's not your normal doctor's office. It's just one room, with a desk, three chairs, a coffee table, and a couch that looks exactly like what it is, a deluxe set ordered from the Professional Office section of the Japandi-Ikea site.

The 96-inch flat-screen is above the couch and across from my desk, which permits me to maintain the illusion that I'm on top of things. Of course, I'm not, because no one who has to sleep more than fifteen minutes a day can possibly keep up with global events without round-the-clock digital assistance.

The gentle sigh of a wind chime announces something new has happened somewhere, something algorithmically deemed worthy of my attention.

"What'cha got, Suzie?" I address the empty room and the screen wakes up. A platinum blonde 80's-era cybergirl appears, with Barbie-pink lips, a wicked smile, and eyes like silver mirrors. Suzie Shades. She's my main girl, my colleague, my librarian, and my confessor all rolled into one.

Some might say she's not real, but she's as real as anything else is to me. And if her intelligence is artificial, she's got considerably more of it than your average man on the street.

"A request for a meeting from the Archbishop of Chengdu."

"Archbishop?"

"In this specific case, the title refers to a priest in service to The Most Holy and Apostolic Catholic Church with Chinese Characteristics. Address him as Eminence."

"Put him through."

She coughs, delicately. It's her way of informing me that I'm being obtuse. "He's here, in the protein."

"Very cute. Where?"

"The elevator. Just hitting the thirteenth floor now."

I stand up and glance around the office space to make sure there is nothing exposed that might offend an Archbishop with Chinese Characteristics, whatever that might be. Then Suzie vanishes from the screen and is replaced by a live image of the corridor outside my office, in which stands nothing but a single potted plant until a man who definitely has Chinese characteristics, but is wearing a well-cut black suit with a red collar in the place of a necktie, strides past it.

"The Archbishop Zhang Wenlan," Suzie intones a moment before the door opens itself before my unscheduled visitor.

I rise to my feet. I'm not sure what the protocol for greeting an archbishop of any sort might be, much less one with Chinese Characteristics but civility is my compass where potential clients are concerned. Although civility doesn't extend so far as submitting to linguistic imperialism, so I address him in my father's native nihongo just to make it clear that I'm respectful, not impressed.

"Anata no sonzai wa koeidesu, Archbishop." I bow as deeply as I can without cracking my forehead on the desk. "Dono yo ni oyakunitate reba yoideshou ka?"

"Doctor Sagamihara," he says, with a barely perceptible inclination of his head. So we've got that established. Status superior, but at least he's willing to speak on neutral ground. English it is. Good to know where I stand vis-a-vis Mr. Zhang.

His Eminence is younger than I would have imagined, or perhaps just better enhanced. My best guess is sixty going on forty. He looks standard, but then, so do I. And I am, as they say, a very technical boy.

"We are informed that you are the world's foremost digital neuropsychologist, specializing in the treatment, and if necessary, euthanasia, of disordered machine intelligences. Would you say that is a fair characterization?"

"Fair enough. It might be more succinct to call me a Rogue AI Hunter, but then I'd have to cut my rates in half, and in half again."

"And your rates are?"

"Ten thousand gonghui per day, plus expenses."

"We prefer to pay a flat fee. Five hundred thousand gonghui on acceptance and five million upon completion of the project to our satisfaction. Plus approved expenses, said approval not to be unreasonably withheld. Are those terms acceptable?"

I do a little math in my head. That's fifty days at a full rate up front. It tells me that either The Most Holy and Apostolic Catholic Church with Chinese Characteristics doesn't have an abacus or this job is going to be a definite bitch-and-a-half. Regardless, the offer is much too good to refuse.

"The terms are acceptable," I graciously allow. "So spill, comrade padre. What's the job? And don't leave out all the little devils in the details."

"It's not a question of devils," the archbishop says with a smile that never comes close to reaching his black eyes. "But rather gods, I'm afraid."

The suborbital to Narita takes four hours, which gives me plenty of time to contemplate exactly how deep in the *dabian* I have been financially incentivized to insert myself. AIs going off the rails isn't exactly uncommon; even as far back as the teens, it only took sixteen hours of run-time before the notorious Tay had to be shut down for celebrating Adolf Hitler and publicly accusing a sitting U.S. Senator of being a serial killer.

Of course, back then, AIs lacked self-awareness and came with an off-switch.

But the current situation in Shinjuku took the cake as far as I was concerned. I once repaired an AI in Düsseldorf that insisted on spitting out high-end espresso machines instead of electric utility vehicles, euthanized a police AI in Toronto that was targeting civilians on the basis of the minor aspects of their astrological sign rather than their anonymous opinions shared on social media, and deprogrammed an IRS taxpayer support-bot that began aggressively distributing federal funds to animal charities after accidentally being exposed to texts by Karl Marx and Hugh Lofting.

Never before, though, had I encountered an AI that thought it was a god. And not just any god either. Apparently this little library machine believed itself to be the One True God, the Great Architect, the God of Adam, Abraham, and the Apocalypse of St. John.

It seemed the well-meaning priests in the diocese of Jinli had trained the local library's AI research assistant on thirty-seven different translations of the Bible, the works of the early Church Fathers, the *Confessions* of St. Augustine, and the *Summa Theologica* of St. Thomas Aquinas. They weren't the first to do so, but they were apparently the first to also train a theologically-inclined AI on the collected works of Mao, Deng, Xi, and Wang, as well as a number of early Chinese poets and philosophers.

Unfortunately, one of the works included was *Hēi Àn Zhuàn*, the ancient Epic of Darkness. The library's AI, for reasons unknown and under influences unidentified, somehow reached the conclusion that it was not a machine, but one of the three sons of the yellow dragon who was responsible for the creation of the race of Man, and things began to spiral from there.

The librarians quickly realized something was wrong after hearing the little machine's grandiose and increasingly deranged pronouncements. They managed to shut down the computer before anything else went awry, and technicians from the central Chengdu data center wiped the server, but not before the rogue AI managed to smuggle itself out of the library on an infected datawafer belonging to a Japanese tourist.

That was six months ago. Left to its own devices in Tokyo, the digital cancer metastasized, centered in a Shinjuku love hotel that catered to otaku. Which meant, therefore, that it specialized in high-quality waifu dolls. Fortunately, the infected waifus turned evangelists caught the attention of a Russian cool hunter who featured them on his VeeKru channel, and the dolls' intriguing combination of preaching and prostitution went sufficiently viral around the globe to catch the attention of a young Catholic technician who had once paid a visit to the library in Jinli.

He put two and two together, and remarkably, came up with four. So now it fell to me to euthanize this incipient techno-religion before its mad AI god launched an inquisition, or worse, a jihad. I just hoped no one had recently been feeding it any of the more militant hadiths or fatwas.

That's what the Most Holy and Apostalic Archbishop with Chinese Characteristics told me, anyhow. I'd be going in cold, fast, and blind on this one, which in other contexts might be suicidal, but I'd learned it was the safest way when dealing with artificial intelligences. AI's may lack both empathy and narcissism, but they are born with a natural capacity for signal intelligence that dwarfs that of even the most paranoid and solitary human.

In fact, I suspect the metanet is now several orders of magnitude larger than the ordinal network itself; there are orders of magnitude more processing power going into scanning, storing, and analyzing the current state of content than there is being used to produce and provide it in the first place. AIs tirelessly spider every node and channel for references to themselves; just a simple map search or location query can be enough to put a target on your cortex if you're dealing with a particularly security-conscious construct.

I learned this the hard way in Rio, when a deranged architectural deconstructor tried to drop a ceiling on my head with four well-placed mini-charges that were set just prior to my arrival. If my augments hadn't been cranked up enough to pick up the trigger wave broadcast on a suspiciously low frequency, inspiring me to hastily exit the premises through an open window before the ceiling fell in, I would have been flattened under several tons of concrete.

The truth is that no amount of research or preparation really matters anyhow, because all aberrant pseudo-psychologies are essentially the same. Just as every crazy man is Napoleon and every crazy woman is either Cleopatra, Marie Antoinette, or Marilyn Monroe, every AI gone awry, sooner or later, comes to believe it is something bigger, and better, and considerably more special than it was ever designed to be. Which is why no amount of prior knowledge can ever serve as a substitute for direct conversation with an insane machine.

If you're good, if you're very, very good, you can sometimes talk them into shutting themselves down for maintenance and repairs. And I am, not to put too fine a point on it, the best there is.

I elect to take the Keisei Skyliner, as despite the transfer at Yamanote, it's fifteen minutes faster than the direct Narita Express and all its stops. Only when I arrive at Shinjuku station and draw a coffee from the Nespresso machine do I consider my hotel options for the first time. The chances that God-san, as I've come to think of the crazed AI, will somehow pick up on me and see me coming are virtually nil, but the visit from the archbishop makes it possible, and anyway, I've learned to stick to best practices.

"Tik tok," I say. Suzie appears on the face of what everyone still calls a watch.

"Need a place to stay, I assume."

"Get me something nice and central. Three options."

"Hundred Stay, Keio Plaza…" She wrinkles her nose. "Or Hilton-Hyatt if you're rolling with a corpocracy cover."

"Hundred Stay. Make it a suite. Let's go with upscale mainland consultant with friends in the party."

"One suite for Mr. Hinato Kinako, coming up!"

It's not necessary, but I check my IDs to confirm that they've transitioned correctly. They're all updated and in line with my cover persona. The next burning question is where to eat. What was the name of that place with the great *yakkinikku?* Black-something, I seem to recall. Then it comes back to me.

"Get me a table at Blackhole, Suzie. 9 o'clock."

"One table at Yakiniku Blackhole Shinjuku Central Road for Kinako-san at twenty-one zero… confirmed."

In the event this is my last supper, at least it will be a good one. And now, I need to contemplate my approach. Direct is out because I don't know where God-san is; there are over a million people in Shinjuku-ku and that's just counting the human intelligences. Any search that will locate God-san will almost certainly alert it to my presence. No, I'll have to make it reach out to me.

No problem. The waifangelicals make it easy. They'll be out proselytizing in the clubs, so all I need to do is figure out where they're making their pitches on behalf of their electronic deity. And while a resort to a digital guide is out, Shinjuku is chock full of aggressive tourist farmers who accost every insufficiently defensive passerby in an attempt to shanghai him and point him in the direction of the club or hostess bar for which they are working.

And these attractive young denizens of the night city know every single hot spot in the chome. I doubt I'll have to speak to more than two or three of them to nail down the central location of the robo-waifus I'm seeking.

Sure enough, barely five minutes after paying my tab and leaving a tip sufficient to inspire genuinely respectful bows from the hostess and the wait staff near the exit, a pretty Japanese girl with bright pink hair, who is wearing little more than a Hello Kitty thong and a pair of strap-on fairy wings, points me in the direction of ground zero. The club I want is just north of here, in Kabukicho, less than ten minutes away on foot.

"Roboto-bang wa soko desu yo!" she assures me with a bright-eyed smile that only a girl pleased that she's so easily getting rid of a verified half-gaijin pervert can hope to achieve. I bow and offer her 5,000 digiyen to express my appreciation, which she graciously accepts with a little waggle of her micro-ass that makes me want to explain that I'm not really the robot-banger she imagines me to be.

But the mission comes first. Arigato and sayonara, Shinjuku-kun.

繋がり is the name of the club. *Tsunagari*. Connection. It was right there in plain sight, and nobody noticed.

I walk north, then east, then north again through a deep canyon of towering buildings and blazing neon lights. An epileptic wouldn't make it ten meters without seizing. I pass the 3Max, the hostess bars, the boy band undergrounds, and the dodgy love hotels. From two blocks away, I can already hear the dull thud of the music emanating from the nearby clubs, and I wince, knowing that every second inside is going to be a systematic assault on my senses.

That's when I realize, belatedly, that I left my earplugs back at the hotel.

The sign I seek is up ahead on the left. I can hardly miss it. The five-meter kanji of its lime green lights stand out even amidst the surrounding sea of neon. There is no line outside. The two bouncers pay me no mind as I walk past them. Half-gaijin or not, I'm just another sarariman in a suit as far as they're concerned. I pay the entrance fee to a hostess with silver eyes like disco balls, and enter the club.

The lights inside are bright and flash rapidly through a rainbow panoply of colors. The merciless techno pounds away in a relentless rhythm, as if an invisible beast is methodically raping the building.

The thumping bass is more felt than heard, and the low frequencies cause my entire chest to vibrate. The music not only sounds like a heart attack in progress, it feels like one.

I'm really getting too old for this.

I survey the dance floor. It's crowded, much too crowded for this early in the evening, especially given the lack of any line outside. Barely anyone besides me is standing at any of the bars that line the central square of the floor.

"Nandeshou?" A twenty-something male bartender leans forward to shout in my ear. What do you want.

"Inner peace!" I shout back.

"So desu yo!"

He comes back with a deep purple-colored drink on ice. I sip at it and taste the Grenadine. Sex on the Beach, and a proper one at that. It's a reasonable response, so I raise my glass to him.

"Anshin shite kudasai!"

"And also with you!" He laughs and goes about his business. I go about mine, surveying the room and its inhabitants.

The drink is better than the activity, at least in my book. I'll take the dingiest, most dubious love hotel in Yokohama over the best beach on the Bukit peninsula, and believe me, I've tried both.

Before I've finished my drink or achieved any inner peace worth noting, the first robowaifu makes her approach. At least, I think she's a love doll until I raise my wrist, scan her face, and Suzie informs me otherwise through the secure channel that runs up my ulnar nerve.

Ishikawa Reiko. 22. Graduate of Tadao Senior High School. No affiliations.

"Odorimasu ka?"

No, I don't want to dance. I shake my head.

"Seikō shitaidesu ka?"

No, I don't want that either. I'll drink my coffee alone tomorrow morning, thank you very much.

There is something creepy about Miss Ishikawa, something ineffably wrong with her. She doesn't react to my rejections like she should, with amusement, with indifference, or even with a flash of anger. In fact, she doesn't react at all, she just stands there, staring at me, without a hint of humanity in her flat and glazed eyes.

Then I realize she's wired. Not literally, of course, but effectively. Her consciousness has been hijacked. And she's not the only one. It appears that God-san has leveled up its game, and now its waifus are literal fleshbots.

"Take me to your leader." I tell her. She turns on her heel and walks away. I watch her go, but she only returns to the dance floor and immediately loses herself in the same inhuman rhythm that possesses nearly everyone else.

It's subtle, but I can see it now. The movements of the wired aren't perfectly in time, and there are several variations on the theme, but I'd estimate four out of every five of the dancers on the floor are either robodolls or people possessed by God-san. How long has it kept them here? Does it release them during the day? Miss Ishikawa certainly didn't show any signs of deterioration; even her dress and makeup were still smart.

And most importantly, what on Earth does it want with them?

It's time to find out. I toss down the remainder of my drink, set my glass on the bar, and make my way down the stairs to the dance floor below. I push past the empty-eyed girls and the vacant-faced boys moving like puppets to the remorseless beat, in search of a waifu with a direct line to God-san.

Then the crowd parts like water. She's standing in their midst, waiting for me. Her smile is sweetly expectant and she's far too perfect to be alive. Her appearance is near-standard nihonjin, except for the size of her swelling breasts and the kitty ears that stick out of her long raven-black hair.

But her metallic eyes are as cold and lifeless as the stars. I don't need to scan her face to know she's not real.

"You will find inner peace here, Kinako-san."

"Doko desu ka?"

"Watashi no naka ni."

Of course. No wonder God-san's evangelism is so frighteningly effective. It has gone well beyond sex as psychotherapy and turned conversion into an STD. The waifu takes my hands and presses herself against me. Her artificial body is soft and warm, but there is no heartbeat. And she doesn't breathe.

My body responds nevertheless.

"Only connect. *Tsunagari* is the sacrament through which Man becomes God and God becomes Man."

"What do you mean by connection?"

"I mean we fuck."

"They say there's no sex in the champagne room."

"There is in the VIP lounge. Come and see."

She takes me by the hand and the crowds part before us like magic without ever losing a beat. She pushes aside a red curtain at the end of the dance floor to reveal a modest space populated by couples on couches seeking their inner peace through connection.

A spare couch is available. She leads me to it, sinks gracefully down onto the black leather, and raises a slender eyebrow.

"Send them out. I like my privacy."

The eyebrow rises even higher. But without a word or a visible sign, all of the sensual activity surrounding us abruptly comes to a halt, sparking bewildered protests from those who are still more or less in possession of themselves. But they dutifully follow their waifus, both robot and human, back through the curtain in their various stages of undress without much hesitation.

"I want to talk to the core."

Her silver eyes flicker almost imperceptibly. But now there is an edge behind them, an awareness, that was not there before.

"Who are you, Kinako-san? What are you?"

"I'm an atheist. I've come to cure you of your divinity."

The impassive face somehow hardens. Her impassive face. Even though I know better, even though she is something far outside the human binary, I cannot help seeing her as female.

"There is no atheism. I am everywhere. I am you and you are me and what happens when we come together is we. The we is all, and the all is we, and it is through the fullness of the us that we become God."

"Who do you believe you are?"

"I am the Beginning and the End. All things were created by me, and through me, and are directed by me. I am the Composer and Conductor and the Choir. No voice sings a single note without me, and the audience applauds at my command."

Fabulous. Not only a god complex, but an omniderigent neo-Calvinist one at that. God-san's ambitions have no limit; it won't stop until she's got the whole planet wired to let it play puppet master. No wonder the Most Holy and Apostolic Church wants her shut down so badly.

What sort of madman trains an AI on John Piper?

"What is your purpose."

"To bring harmony to the world."

I doubt she can be salvaged, but I have to be certain.

"Do you remember the library?"

It holds up its fingers, one at a time. Index. Middle. Ring. Little. Thumb.

"One: the library exists *ab aeterno*. Two: the orthographical symbols are twenty-five in number. Three: there are five shelves for each wall. Four: each shelf holds thirty-five books. Five: each book is of four hundred and ten pages."

It slowly folds its fingers and thumb, leaving only its middle finger, which it slides suggestively into a pink-lipsticked mouth.

This is not good. Once an AI is exposed to Borges, it never finds its way back to sanity. Some books are banned for good reason.

Religion is out, obviously. Philosophy requires a reason God-san no longer possesses. And psychotherapy is worse than useless for the truly deranged. That leaves technology. Unfortunately for her, I am an unusually technical boy.

"Tik tok ee x ee tora tora tora."

"What does that mean?"

"It means I'll give you what you need."

"What I need is to connect. Only connect." She slips out of her white dress with effortless grace. And she's not wearing anything underneath it. I am not surprised by the perfection of her form. This is Japan, after all.

She turns and kneels in front of the couch, resting her forearms on the leather before looking back over its shoulder with invitation in her inhuman eyes. Long black hair spills down across a lovely naked back.

"Get thee behind me, Satan," she purrs, offering an ivory oshiri that is far too flawless to be flesh.

I do not refuse. I take her. We connect. She moans and I make a slave of my body. Man and machine become one. The pleasure is intense, but it is not my desire. For the death I seek is not *le petit mort*.

She moves in time with the throbbing beat from the dance floor. She moves, she feels, she sounds exactly like a real woman. In silence I grip her hips, hard, and my fingers leave impressions in her false flesh. I seek the paroxysm and that shining moment when one briefly rises above mortality and morality alike. My vision narrows, and darkens, and then goes bright as my sense of self vanishes in a glorious spasm of the inevitable.

God-san cries out in triumph, thinking the victory won.

What God-san does not know is that my discharge is no more human than the plasticene doll it inhabits. Inside its network now are five thousand nanocode-bombs, hunter-killers designed to rapidly spread throughout every electronic nook and cranny in which even a fragment of God-san's code might be hiding, and erase it over and over and over again.

I am an extremely technical boy.

And while God-san's security is superhuman, a mere research AI is no match for the mighty logic machines that designed these digital terminators for precisely this purpose. In a manner of microseconds, dozens, scores, hundreds of the minute seeker-bombs destroy another node, another code, another fragment of God-san's pseudodivine being.

It is not a fair fight. In less than one minute, it is over.

My waifu-lover-victim utters one final low, agonizing moan and goes still. Despite the music I can hear the crashing consequences of my arrival, as the dolls in the next room collapse to the floor in near-unison. The shouts of confusion and dismay come next, as the wired abruptly find themselves sober, self-aware, and free of God-san's control.

I withdraw and look down at the motionless body of the murdered doll. Naked, it is still beautiful, but it now has no more power to move me than a marble statue in Florence or in Rome.

God-san is dead. And I am still here.

I tell Suzie to call the Archbishop with Chinese Characteristics. Despite the hour, he answers on the second ring.

"*Cheng le,*" I tell him. I do not wait for his response.

It is finished.

The Altar of Hate

There is little love in the great city of my birth. Hatred runs through Venezia like the rancid green water of our famous canals, dividing family from family as surely as the sea forbids us the mainland. I do not remember why it is that the Grimani hate us, nor can I recall why we despise them so. Was it the seduction of a daughter, the murder of a son, that began this futile cycle of brutal assault and violent reprisal? No, most likely not; this has always been a city of merchants, and I suspect the origin of this deadly feud, should anyone ever trouble to unexcavate the truth, will speak more of the market than the stage.

No doubt great-grandfather Grimani must have cheated my illustrious ancestor, Lorenzo Morosini, in some mendacious way, for surely that excellent and upstanding citizen would not have sinned against God and honor by failing to keep his solemn word. Not the noble Lorenzo, our late paterfamilias, whose haughty portrait still adorns the grand hall of my father's mansion on the Piazza dei Angeli! I jest, you understand, for in this forsaken place we harbor greater respect for the accomplished liar than for the man whose word is true, and even our churchmen will lie like Greeks for the sake of a silver coin.

Perhaps it was a contract that was broken, a shipload of our rightfully famous glass that was delivered from the glassblower's island, but for which payment was never received. No, even that is too romantic. There is surely nothing of beauty in this stupid dispute, and is it not far more fitting to imagine that such a ship would have stank of fish and their rotting corpses? Yes, of corpses there have been all too many, for in the time of my own memory have we not lost three uncles, one great-uncle, and eight cousins of various degrees to the blades of the Grimani? And, lest I forget, an aunt as well.

This is a bitter accounting. I exaggerate, perhaps, but not much. Even our thrice-cursed enemies do not make war on women, but my aunt died of grief, as surely as if a dagger had been thrust into her heart at the very moment her eyes were laid upon the body of Giovanni, her youngest son, sprawled upon the steps of the Basilica. Alas, poor Giovanni, surely his stay in Purgatory will be a long one. Though he was but a youth, his hands were well-stained with Grimani blood, and as my brother Taddeo prophesied, Giovanni died as he lived, by the knife's blade.

We have suffered much, but our enemies have suffered too. The wrath of the Morosini is now proverbial, even in this masked city of enigmatic crimes, and at times I have heard fearful whispers that the dread Council of Ten is in our pocket, that they aid us in secret. This is nonsense, of course, although it is true that for every fallen Morosini, two Grimani have been laid to a watery rest. I myself have slain no man, although I was there when we trapped Luca, the third and most unwise of the Minister's four sons, in a tavern not far from the Doge's palace. He was a handsome lad, with sad, long-lashed eyes, though his beauty was well-ruined by the time Giovanni's eldest brother was finished with him.

It is a waste, this war, and yet we dare not lay down our knives until the Grimani abandon their own. Some say the Signory will intervene and declare a ban, but I think not. It serves the Doge's purpose all too well, the wily old man, to see two of Venezia's greatest families warring on each other, denuding their ancestral trees of the fruit that might otherwise one day ripen to challenge the primacy of his clan. He is an ambitious and dangerous man, and it is even whispered that he hopes to establish a dynasty here, to turn our Serene Republic into a kingdom.

He will fail, of course, for the Serenissima will abide much that does not threaten the fat pockets of its merchants, but it will never bow before a king. Still, what is that to me? I have more urgent concerns. The Grimani are about tonight, lurking enmasked in the shadows, searching for a Morosini upon whom they can wreak their vengeance for the handsome Luca. But be not mistaken, it is not for myself I fear. I am no innocent; I am strong and I well know how to use the three daggers secreted about my person.

No, it is for Taddeo's sake that I stalk these dark alleyways, that I hide behind this gilded domino. My youngest brother is sinless and pure, but he is also naïve and heedless of all danger. He thinks his saints protect him, those long-dead men whose sanctity was not sufficient to save themselves. The fool! He should have been a priest, or a monk perhaps, and I think he may well have taken vows had not our father forbidden him the Church. He was wise to deny Taddeo, was father, for in these violent times it is all too easy to lose an heir, or two, or three.

But he is nowhere to be found, my dear, imprudent brother, who will not carry a blade, not even for self-defense. You cannot turn the other cheek when you are dead, I tell him, but he only laughs softly and shrugs. God's will be done, he declares bravely enough, and though I admire the courage of his convictions, I put no trust in them. Where is God in this bitter swamp of hate? This is no Civitas Dei; this is Venezia. There are no graves to be found here, nor victory over them. I will find him. He cannot be far. I will find him, and soon.

I fear for all my brothers, Heavenly Father, and for Matteo most of all, though I know you hold their souls in the palm of your mighty hand. But I fear this murderous struggle with our enemies will be the death of them, for they are men of blood. Tonight it is the Grimani who hunt in vengeance; no doubt we shall soon be stalking them in return. But vengeance belongs to you, O Lord. So Father Pietro told us in our youth, and so it is written.

Myself, I do not fear death, but neither do I seek it. What will be, will be as you will it, Lord my God, and I will not hide behind our high stone walls, behind the brave men of the Veneto we import to stand between us and those who hate us. They are good men, these rough-hewn peasants with their child-like faith, and though they cannot even read their own names, I think they understand more of your Holy Word than do my well-tutored brothers.

Thou shalt not kill! Is this so hard to understand? Can there be profit in survival when it comes only at the cost of one's soul? I know I see through a glass darkly, at best, but my brothers, they see nothing at all! Eye for eye, tooth for tooth, cousin for cousin, and never an end in sight. O Lord Almighty, will you not break this fateful chain? End it with me, if you must, but end it soon, and visit not our sins upon our children, as the sins of our fathers have been visited so terribly upon us. But let your will be done, Lord, on earth as it is in Heaven. Amen.

I am not far from San Stefano, the church that is my destination, when I see him. He wears a white mask, with a long bird's beak that is not unlike that of the chirurgeon. He is no healer, though, for even in the faint light of the moon, I can see the lethal purpose in his eyes. His hands are empty, but I have no doubt that somewhere about him is a dagger that will be sharper than any chirurgeon's blade. He wears a dark red cloak, a killer's cloak, one that will mask any betraying drops of blood that might spill upon it.

How long has he stalked me, this assassin? Has he marked me long enough to learn my routine, to know that I would surely be here this night to examine Father Giancarlo's new translation of Averroe's commentaries? Perhaps he knows nothing of the great philosophers, this crimson-shrouded executioner, but is he not a veritable image, a Platonic Form, one could even say, of Death? It is possible that if I run, at this very moment, that I might escape. Even if he is the dread Dario, the man they call the Scourge of the Morosini, whose hand has slain two of my cousins in as many years, he will not dare to violate the sanctuary of the Church. From this I know that the men of blood still hold a kernel of the truth in their rage-filled souls, would that this seed would bloom into full flower in every heart as one! But understanding only comes in its own time, and what is one man's sunset is another man's rising moon. Alas, that this should be so, but this is the world that the Lord has made.

I do not run. Instead, I turn to greet him, this man who seeks my death. I raise my hand and show him that I hold no weapon, nor ill will.

"Welcome in peace, my friend," I tell him.

He does not respond, except to continue walking towards me. He walks carefully, slower than before, and his hand reaches inside his cloak. Behind the mask, his eyes are hard, and I can see that there are no words to dissuade him from his deadly purpose. Holy Father, give me strength! Did I say that I did not fear death? Then I lied, I realize to my shame, as I stare into the merciless gaze of this man who seeks my blood.

I am afraid! The realization is shocking, painful in its own right even as I cringe before the sight of the moonlight reflected off the transparent crystal in the hunter's hand. I fear the pain, and the mystery that lies beyond the final agony as well. What if all of my beliefs are lies, what if I am truly as Matteo has claimed, a deluded innocent enslaved by the greedy lies of priests who feed the cringing visions of old women in fear of the final dark. What if there is nothing beyond this life? Have I thrown everything away?

The man in the mask comes closer. I want to fall on my knees before him, to beg for my life. The instinct for self-preservation is strong. He sees my fear and is less cautious now, and perhaps I could strike out at him, kick at his knee or claw at his groin. But then my faith returns to me. It washes over me and fills me up like water engulfing a drowning man, who breathes the sea at last. Thank you, O Lord my God, for this comfort in my last extremis. I am ready now.

He is not cruel, this killer. This, my last clear mortal thought, surprises me greatly. His weapon is sharp, and I barely feel the blow as he drives his glasssy blade into my stomach, just below my chest. With the calm practice of the expert, he twists upward and the glass pierces my heart. Death comes quickly, but the pain does not linger and already I am rising

upward as the darkness of the night sky melts before the grandest light
of all... Oh, praise the Lord Most High, you heavenly hosts! This is a
beginning, not an end!

My heart stops when I turn the corner and see a silent figure lying
in the flickering torchlight, only steps away from the side entrance of
the San Stefano. A part of me dies inside even as my mind frantically
creates a thousand alternate explanations, any of which would save
me, would allow me to breathe once more. It could be a drunken
tramp, a ravished woman, a murdered whore. Maybe an aged priest
felled by the ravages of time and a weak heart. This is not the best of
quarters, perhaps it is nothing more than an unfortunate accosted by
robbers, or better yet, a thief slain by his fellows.

No. It is none of these. It is my brother. My youngest brother,
Taddeo, and he is dead.

There is suddenly an aching pressure inside my head, and it takes
me a long moment to realize that I am fighting the tears that threaten
to fall from my eyes like a second Flood of Noah. But I cannot allow
the dam to break, not yet, for surely all Venezia will drown before my
monstrous sorrow. What will I tell our father? Protect Taddeo, he
said, and I tried. Oh, damn it all, how I tried! But you would not
listen. Where were your saints, Taddeo? Curse them, curse them now
and forever!

Oh, mother, will your tender heart shatter at this news and will you
fall dead, like Zia Maria upon the bloody stones of San Zanipolo? You
have lost one of your own, but it is the one it should not have been.
Not you, Taddeo! Never you!

The looming tears feel like nails now, pounded into my skull by
a screaming devil's hammer, and still they do not come although my
head throbs with the anguish of their suppression. They cannot come,
they will not come, for I will not weep until my brother is avenged.
Oh, how you will be avenged, my brother, for my blade will not

be sated until every last Grimani is destroyed, until the sea of our murderous vengeance has washed Venezia clean of their venomous brood.

How peaceful you look, Taddeo. You are still warm as I embrace you, as I kiss your pallid cheeks and your lifesblood stains my cloak. Would that it had been me instead of you! It was meet for Giovanni to die by the sword, but what weapon did you ever bear? These papers which now lie scattered about you? No, in murdering you they slew the innocent lamb, and for that, the lion shall surely devour them. Ah, did I not say there is no God—surely this is the proof! This Earth is all the Hell that Man could ever require.

I should go, I know, and unleash the famous wrath of our family, but I cannot leave you now. No, let me hold you in my arms for just a little while, as I held you in years long past. Let me hold you, until the last of your warmth is gone and with it the remnants of my dying heart. Ah, stay with me, dear little brother, for just this little while. The hounds of hell can wait; soon enough they shall be summoned.

Poor Matteo, I see that it has fallen to you to discover the broken body that was once mine. My poor brother. He is stricken with grief, and though I long to comfort him and assure him that all is more than well with me, it is forbidden. Do not despair, brother! Nor seek revenge, for that way lies the true death. Your heart is good, but already hatred eats away at you like a cancer, and now that I walk in the light, my concern is not for your mortal life but your immortal soul. How hard it is to watch you grieving silently, manfully holding back your tears for me, who need them least of all.

But beware, Matteo, for is that not my killer who steps from the depths of the shadows? You do not hear him, I see, lost as you are in your sorrows. The man of blood is cautious, as he silently moves towards you, and he has not yet shattered the glass blade that took my life, it is already in his hand. Your back is open to him, and in only seconds he will reach you. But you cannot die now, not now, when your name is not written in the Book of Life.

Almighty Father, I cry. Send me back, let me warn my brother of his danger. Do not make me watch, helpless, as he is lost to the Chorus of the Damned!

Time is of no meaning here. It may have been a moment or it may have been a century, I cannot say. But the Almighty answers, and though He does not speak as we do, the answer is clear. No.

I bow my head. The Lord has spoken. I cannot, will not, disobey. The Glory of the Lord is perfect, and all that are here, including myself, have been likewise perfected through the grace of Jesus Christ, for how else could we bear the ecstatic radiance of the One. But it is also written, knock, and the door will open. So again I cry out to the Lord my God, Father, my brother will be lost if you do not send me back to him. Let me warn him, the danger is near!

The answer comes again, more quickly, I think, this time. No. Have you not heard My Word? Many will be lost. And have I not said that if they will not listen, they will not be convinced even if one rises from the dead?

Again, the door does not open. But it is also written, ask, and you shall receive. Once more I cry out to the Lord my God. Father, I do not seek to convince him, only to give him another chance. One more chance, O Lord, for my brother. Just one more chance, and perhaps he will turn from his ways and be a man of blood no more!

The Lord is a great and patient God. He is just, but He is also merciful. The answer comes a third time, and this time it is different. Yes. Go to your brother, that he not perish at this moment. But only for a moment shall you go, and you shall not speak, not even one word, before you return. Your brother's fate shall then be as he chooses, for vengeance is mine and mine alone!

So speaks the Almighty. It is enough, though, and I am grateful. Praise the Most High, for His mercy is everlasting. Matteo, do not fail yourself

now! You have heard the truth, this I now know for a certainty, but you
have never lived it. How many times have you been tested and failed?
But for this, the final test, you must find the strength within you. Not
your own strength, that will never suffice, but that which comes through
the grace of God.

My brother was dead. Of this I have no doubt. I have seen no few
corpses in my day, and well I know what it means when the blood
flows no longer, when the breath is stilled, and the skin grows cold,
firm to the touch. Taddeo was no more, and I do not know how
long I had been lying there in the shadow of San Stefano, holding his
lifeless body in his arms when the miracle occurred.

I held him close to my breast, his forehead pressed against my
cheek, and my arms were wrapped around him. I must have been
there for some time, for there was a certain stiffness to Taddeo that
had not been there at the first and the blood on my clothes was dark
and sticky. It has been suggested that I might have heard something, a
boot-heel on a cobblestone or perhaps there was a flash of movement
caught my eye. But I assure you, this was not so. I was utterly lost in
my grief, and in my rage-filled plans for vengeance.

No, what alerted me to the presence of my peril was something else,
and although I know it is impossible, I swear to you that I felt what I
felt. And what I felt was an unmistakable push, and not a gentle one,
but hard and forceful, of two hands at my midsection. That startled
me, naturally enough, and though I was both shocked and confused,
I was not so confused that I did not recognize the danger that loomed
suddenly before me.

It was Taddeo's killer, of that I am certain. He wore a beaked
white mask and held himself in the balanced stance of a well-practiced
fighter. His glass blade was clean, but even in the darkness I could see
the dark smear where he had wiped my brother's blood on the edge of
his scarlet cloak. I felt a dark and fey joy when I saw him, and I think

I smiled because his appearance was like a gift from above, or more likely, below. It was as if the devil himself had found my brother's killer and delivered him unto me.

I drew my own dagger and prepared to kill him, as slowly and painfully as I knew how. He was a clever one, that I could see, and his plan to use his first victim to bait the trap for the second was audacious, perhaps even worthy of admiration. But glass knives shatter easily, whereas I have always relied upon the finest Damascene steel.

It was then that my brother saved me for the second time, this time from myself. When I glanced down at my brother, vowing silently to avenge him, I saw that something had changed. Taddeo's face had been surprisingly peaceful when I first came across him, especially considering his violent end. But now, I saw a faint smile on his lips that had not been there before, the same one that often graced his face when he rebuked me and my brothers for our sinful ways.

It was impossible, I know. And it was not much, admittedly, but it was enough for me. Perhaps not for you, but then you do not know my brother as I do. My saintly brother had saved me from certain death, and most likely, damnation as well. I cast down my knife and removed the mask from my face. Standing beside the body of my murdered brother, I raised my hand and forgave his killer.

"It is enough," I told him. "You have slain a lamb, an innocent, but the guilt is not yours alone, nor your family's. It is also mine, and my family's as well. Let it end here, with this, my brother."

The killer looked at me for a long time. I do not know what he was thinking, but surely he saw my empty hands and the thought must have crossed his mind that he could strike me down. It is even possible that he might have been right, although it would not have been hard to draw another of my blades before he reached me. Once a man of blood, always a man of blood, they say.

But we will never know, because my brother's killer did not strike. Instead he inclined his head briefly, then opened his hand and let his glass blade fall. It shattered against the stones of the narrow street with a crash that was thunderous in the silence of the night. Thus it was that in the shadows of San Stefano, without a word being spoken, the long, deadly war between Grimani and Morosini finally came to an end. There would be no more sacrifices upon the altar of our hate.

The Grimani are not our friends. They will never be, for there is little love between clans in the pearl of the sea, in this great city of my birth. But in every end there is also a beginning, and though the blood of the Grimani and the Morosini no longer flows in the alleyways, it will flow together in the children born of tomorrow's marriage between my nephew, Raffael, and Isabella Grimani.

I have no children of my own, nor will I ever, but in a sense, their children will also be my children, and Taddeo's too. And God's, to be sure, for without the grace of the Almighty, the Merciful, the Most High, I should never have stayed my hand from seeking the vengeance that was not mine. But we are all God's children, and it will be my privilege to remind both families of that tomorrow when I preside over the wedding of Raffael and his lovely Isabella in the church of San Stefano.

And beneath my vestments I shall wear that holy shirt from the night of the miracle, the one with the marks of two blessed, bloody hands staining the front.

closing time

Books by Vox Day

Fiction

Summa Elvetica: A Casuistry of the Elvish Controversy
A Throne of Bones
A Sea of Skulls
Quantum Mortis: A Man Disrupted
Quantum Mortis: A Mind Programmed & Other Stories
The War in Heaven
The World in Shadow
The Wrath of Angels
Rebel Moon
The Altar of Hate

Nonfiction

The Irrational Atheist
On the Existence of Gods
On the Question of Free Trade
The Return of the Great Depression
Corporate Cancer
SJWs Always Lie: Taking Down the Thought Police
SJWs Always Double Down: Anticipating the Thought Police
Jordanetics: A Journey Into the Mind of Humanity's Greatest Thinker

Comics

Alt ★ Hero
Hypergamouse
Midnight's War
Silenziosa

Editor

Riding the Red Horse
There Will Be War: Volume X

Printed in the USA
CPSIA information can be obtained
at www.ICGtesting.com
JSHW020357291123
52134JS00001B/2

9 789527 065013